MURDER ON HOLY ISLAND

A LOCKHART AND DEAN MYSTERY

KAY RACE

For Keith, my rock, the love and light of my life.

Whilst seeking revenge,
dig two graves - one for yourself.

Douglas Horton

ALSO BY KAY RACE

Trapped in the Dark Decade

November 2018

Book 1 in The Dark Edinburgh Series

Dark Past, Secret Present

October 2020

Book 2 in The Dark Edinburgh Series

Dark Hearts, Enlightened Souls

May 2021

Book 3 in The Dark Edinburgh Series

Against the Odds

November 2021

Book 1 in The Frobisher Family Saga

Into the Fray

May 2022

Book 2 in The Frobisher Family Saga

Deeds Not Words

October 2022

Book 3 in The Frobisher Family Saga

ABBREVIATIONS

ANPR: automatic number plate recognition

CPS: Crown Prosecution Service

DVLA: Driver and Vehicle Licensing Agency

DWP: Department for Work and Pensions

HMRC: His Majesty's Revenue and Customs

HQ: Head Quarters

MIT: Murder Investigation Team/Major Incident Team

PM: Post Mortem (Examination)

PNC: Police National Computer

POI: Person(s) of Interest

SIO: Senior Investigating Officer

SOCO: Scene of Crime Officer(s) also known as:

CSI: Crime Scene Investigator(s)

PROLOGUE

Saturday 15th July, Edinburgh

The three men sat in the living room of the top floor flat in Melville Terrace, chilled beers in their hands. The window was open in the hope of getting some air into the stifling room as storm clouds gathered and the ominous brooding air reflected the mood of the men sitting around a small occasional table.

John McGuire, who had called the meeting, stood by the open window and gathered his thoughts, the hum of the busy traffic four floors below, barely penetrating his consciousness.

At last he turned round. "Okay guys," he said, getting the attention of the other two, "you both know why we're here."

"Aye," replied Philip Hughes, "to get that pervie bastard since the church is doin' fuck all tae gi'e us any satisfaction."

John frowned at Philip's language and said, "Look Phil, I

know he's messed up your life, but we need to try to be rational if we're going to get justice."

"Well some of us havenae been as lucky as you pal, wi' yer fancy lecturin' job over at the university." He nodded in the direction of George Square on the far side of the expanse of grass and trees known as The Meadows

Martin Davidson, the third man in the room, spoke for the first time, "John's right Phil, we've all suffered the consequences of that man's actions, it's messed with all our lives and relationships."

"Aye, Ah ken that Martin," Phil acknowledged grudgingly, "but at least you two have a salary comin' in at the end o' every month. Ah'm dependin' on punters gettin' intae ma taxi to make ends meet. Some weeks Ah'm workin' sixty plus hours and Ah'm barely makin' ma rent."

"I know," said John, trying to calm down the angry man, "you didn't get the chance to stay on at school or go to college, but we are where we are and we have to look at our options since the Catholic Church has done its usual whitewash job of our complaints against the priest and we know that the Church in America has paid millions in compensation to its victims of abuse by priests."

"A'right then," said Philip challengingly, "what are our options?"

John put his beer on the coffee table. "The first option," he said, tapping his left thumb with his right forefinger, "is to report what Donovan did to the police - as historical abuse."

The other two looked at him dubiously but he continued before they could object, "The police take these allegations seriously and investigate all complaints."

"How dae ye ken for sure?" asked a still belligerent Philip.

"Because," said John, beginning to lose patience, "I made an appointment with Victim Support and I got all the relevant information from them." He picked up some leaflets from the floor beside his chair and handed one to each of them.

"There's something called Criminal Injuries Compensation, that victims of crime can apply for, and it covers mental and emotional injuries too. That might be of particular help to you Phil, in your straitened circumstances."

"It sounds like a good idea Phil," intervened Martin, "I know I have a salary, but with the crippling cost of living and a demanding wife and teenage daughters, I could do with some extra help."

Phil, feeling some hope for the first time, said, "Aye, ye're right enough and maybe there'd be enough tae see a counsellor an' try an' get ma heid sorted. Ah've already lost ma wife an' bairns but maybe there could be some hope for me in the future." He lapsed back into reflective silence as John began to list the second option.

Still counting on his fingers, he said, "A second option, although personally less attractive to me, would be to go to the media and ask for their backing to appeal against the ruling of the Catholic Church and get support in having our complaint upheld. It's not just about the money, we need an acknowledgment of the trauma we've suffered and the effect on our lives ... and we need and deserve an apology. The Catholic Church has to take responsibility for the actions of its priests." He stopped and looked at the others expectantly. They both sat in thought before Martin spoke.

"But that would mean exposing ourselves to public scrutiny, especially when it's something so personal ... and shameful," he added after a pause. He shook his head slowly and went on, "I don't know John, I'm not sure I'd have the courage to deal with that. You know what people are like, they'd say there's no smoke without fire and think maybe we led the priest on."

"Or ask why we never said anything at the time," added Phil.

John held up his hands in a gesture of appeasement and said, "Okay, okay, but I don't see any other options to get us justice for what Fr Donovan did thirty odd years ago." A silence of several minutes followed.

"There is one option ye've no' mentioned John," said Phil quietly, his eyes focused on the floor to avoid their gaze.

"What's that?" the others asked in unison.

"Murder the bastard."

Both John and Martin looked at Phil in shocked disbelief, leaving them slack-jawed.

"You can't be serious Phil!" John eventually exclaimed.

But Phil just looked at his watch and stood up. "Time's money, an empty cab doesnae pay the rent," he said, and left the flat, bringing the meeting to an abrupt end.

1

SATURDAY 16TH SEPTEMBER

Holy Island of Lindisfarne

I t was six forty-five. The sun was just rising behind the Farne Islands, setting the sea alight with a deep orange glow against the purple of the fading night, as the last stars gave way to dawn.

Jessie Grieve was on her way home from her early morning walk with Bertie, her 10 year old whippet and, as she did most days, she stopped by Lindisfarne Priory to take in the glorious sight.

The Castle was a silhouette against the orange and purple which appeared to surround it, halo-like, and she breathed in the crisp air of the early autumn morning. "It's certainly a feast for all the senses," she thought, as she drank in the serenity and listened to the tuneful song of blackbirds, always the first to lead the dawn chorus.

Her meditation was suddenly broken by the pitiful whimpering of Bertie and she pulled herself together, trying to locate where the sound was coming from, worried that the dog had hurt himself. While she had been musing he had wandered off to sniff out the smells left behind by nocturnal creatures.

"Bertie!" she called fretfully, realising that the cries were coming from somewhere in the Priory ruins, then, as she rounded one of the cloisters, she saw Bertie standing rigid, his tail curled so far under him that it reached his tummy. She hurried over, quickly checked him for injuries, then put his lead on, satisfied he wasn't hurt.

"Whatever's the matter?" she asked the trembling dog, stroking his soft brindle fur soothingly. Then her eyes went to where the dog was staring fixedly.

At first she couldn't take in what she was looking at and then her blood turned to ice water as she realised someone was hanging from the darkened cloister. She fumbled in her pocket for the little torch she always carried and, with shaking hands, switched it on.

She gasped in horror as the beam picked out a man's naked body, his eyes bulging and swollen purple tongue protruding from his mouth. Folds of fat hung around his middle, almost obscuring the flaccid penis.

She took an involuntary step back and tried to muster her wits. She pulled her mobile phone from an inside pocket of her jacket and, thankful there was a signal, she called 999.

EIGHTEEN MILES northwest of Holy Island, in the quiet village of Norham, DS Lottie Lockhart came out of her front door and clipped the lead onto the collar of a very excited Dolly who loved her morning walks.

"Which way today Dolly?" she asked her four year old rescue greyhound. Dolly sniffed the crisp autumn air, first in one direction and then another and, having decided, set her pointed nose in her chosen direction and made to cross the road to the path leading down to the river, excited at the thought of the delicious scents left behind by the numerous riverside fauna.

Lottie was waiting patiently whilst Dolly snuffled through what was obviously a very interesting clump of grass when her mobile rang. She knew it was work before she even looked at the caller display as the theme song from "Happy Valley" rang tinnily. She answered, her heart beating faster as she knew it would be something serious to warrant calling this early.

She listened carefully, then replied, "I'm on my way." and hung up. She pulled gently on Dolly's lead as the dog was reluctant to give up her extensive investigation of the long grass.

"Sorry Dolly Dimples, time to go home. Mam has to go to work early today but Jane will take you walkies at lunchtime." On hearing Jane's name, Dolly extricated her head from the grass, sneezed and shook her bedewed nose, then trotted happily alongside her mistress.

Lottie's elderly neighbour, Jane, walked Dolly when Lottie was at work and, if she was going to be late home, she'd feed her and take her into her cottage until Lottie returned. If truth be told, Jane loved Dolly and was always glad to have her company, especially now she was on her own as her husband had died the previous year.

~

JESSIE GRIEVES STOOD SHIVERING, partly from the early morning chill but mainly from shock. The man who had answered her 999 call had been sympathetic but efficient. She was to stay where she was until the first responder arrived at the scene and he told her not to touch the body. "As if!" Jessie thought, shuddering.

She moved a few yards from where the man was hanging and faced the other way, hoping someone would come soon and end this hell she had stumbled upon.

About five minutes later, although it felt like five hours to Jessie, a figure in a high-vis jacket approached her and she almost collapsed with relief to see the familiar face of Dougie White, a Coastguard volunteer who lived on the island.

"Good Morning Mrs Grieves," he said, kindly, "I believe you've had an awful shock this morning." He bent down and stroked Bertie's head and the dog nuzzled the familiar hand affectionately.

"Oh Dougie, Ah'm that glad tae see ye, so Ah am," she said in her broad Northumberland accent, and she began to weep with shock and relief as the big man put an arm around her shoulders, squeezing them gently to comfort her.

She pointed to the cloister and continued, "What a fright Ah got, seeing him hanging there. It was poor Bertie that found him and his whimpering alerted me that something was wrong." She shuddered again and asked, "When can Ah gan home? Ah feel like Ah've been standing here for hours." It was, in fact, only quarter past seven.

"The causeway won't be open until five minutes to eight so they've asked me to secure the scene until the police can get over from the mainland," Dougie replied, taking a roll of tape out of one of the capacious pockets of his coastguard jacket.

The Holy Island of Lindisfarne was cut off from the mainland twice a day by the high tide and members of the Coastguard were often first on the scene in emergencies.

"Why don't you take Bertie home and get yourself a cup of tea and wait there until the police arrive. They'll want to talk to you, as you discovered the body, but I'll direct them to your cottage."

"Aye, thanks Dougie, Ah'll do that son."

"Plenty of sugar, mind!" he called after her, as she quickly led Bertie away from the scene of her horrific discovery.

WHEN LOTTIE ARRIVED at the mainland end of the causeway at seven forty-five she found that two traffic officers in high-vis jackets had been dispatched to take the details of everyone going onto and coming off the island. Although there were still ten minutes before the causeway was officially safe to cross, she saw that some vehicles were already half way over. She opened her car window as one of the officers approached.

"DS Lockhart," she said, holding up her warrant card.

"Ma'am," the officer said, "SOCOs are already at the scene and DC Dean has gone ahead about five minutes ago. You can go over now, but you might want to be careful as some of the causeway still has a shallow covering of water." Lottie nodded her thanks and drove off.

On the island she saw DC Dean's car by the Visitor Centre and she parked behind it, thinking her younger colleague must have been pushing the speed limit to get there before her from his home in Morpeth.

As she donned her crime scene suit and shoe covers she saw there was a marked police car and a white SOCO van which had been parked as close to the Priory as possible without actually entering the grounds.

She walked up to the two police officers guarding the outer perimeter of the scene and, after entering her details in the crime scene log book, they lifted the tape to let her in.

Dean was standing, notebook open, and was already taking a statement from the coastguard. He acknowledged Lottie's arrival with a wave.

Crime scene officers were busily taking photos of the victim and collecting evidence from around the body, where metal plates had been placed on the ground to protect the scene from contamination by everyone who would be attending there over the coming hours and days.

Stepping on them carefully, Lottie approached Tim, the lead CSI, and asked, "Any ID on or around the body Tim?"

"None I'm afraid Lottie," he replied, continuing with his minute inspection of the area under the victim, "but Dougie, the coastguard, thinks he's a retired man who came to live on the island a few months ago, so I'm sure the locals will know more and be happy to tell you."

She was looking at the body with a puzzled expression on her face when Dean came over. He had finished taking the Coastguard's statement and had let the man go home.

"What's that on his chest?" she asked, "it looks like writing of some kind."

Dean, who'd had a preliminary look at the victim when he arrived, said, "Someone, probably the killer, has carved the word *PAEDOPHILE,* as in PAEDO and PHILE under the first part of the word. It looks like it's been done using a fine blade, but we'll have to wait and see what the pathologist has to say about it."

"I take it he's been notified?" Lottie asked.

"He's on his way," replied the DC looking at his watch, "he should be here soon."

As if mentioning his name had conjured him up, the pathologist and his assistant, suited up and carrying metal forensics cases, were walking towards them.

Professor Patrick Healey, known as Paddy to his colleagues, was a genial Irishman nearing retirement who never ceased to show a deep compassion and respect for his victims.

He greeted them solemnly, then looked at the hanging body, any semblance of dignity long gone, and said "Let's get ye down from there ye poor soul an' gi'e ye a wee bit o' dignity." He turned to his pathology assistant, "Alex, gi'e me a hand here please."

While the professor and one of the SOCOs held the body steady, Alex went up the ladder they always brought to a hanging and cut the rope, releasing the deceased. As Alex bagged the rope for any trace evidence, the body was carefully laid on a tarpaulin sheet and Paddy began his preliminary examination.

Paddy Healey had a way of addressing his victims as he went about his first encounter with them and Alex, his assistant, was used to him 'talking' to them as though they were still alive and could hear him.

As he examined the body of the man, he shook his head and said, "To be sure, there's something pitiful, even dehumanising, about the way ye've been stripped, not only o' yer clothes, but yer very identity and strung up like some bloody exhibit."

Meanwhile, a protective tent was erected around the

immediate area of the crime scene to protect it from the elements, as well as any prying eyes of a curious public who would be around once the causeway had opened.

The detectives stood back to give the pathologist room to work while their eyes keenly observed the body. Death, in all its manifestations, was not new to either of them.

Dean looked at the corpse in disgust, as it was lowered to the ground, and he moved away a few paces, unable to bear to look at the hideous sight any longer. Lottie's thoughts, on the other hand, dwelt on how, in her job, they often saw the very worst that humans were capable of.

Some minutes later, Lottie spoke to the pathologist. "I know you hate this question Paddy, but do you have any idea of the time of death?"

"Eight to twelve hours ago Sergeant, but don't hold me to that, I'll have a better idea when I get him back to the morgue," said Paddy, "and he was strangled before being strung up."

He pointed to a ligature mark on the neck that had been obscured by the rope, then he continued, "and can you see the petechial haemorrhaging in the eyes?"

Both detectives murmured assent and Lottie asked, "What about the engraving on his chest? It looks like it was done post mortem."

"Quite right detective," Paddy replied, with a faint smile to acknowledge her observation, "the paucity of blood shows that he was cut after his heart had stopped beating." Then, as an afterthought, he added, "You'll be looking for a small paring knife, or similar, I would say."

"Thanks Paddy, any idea when the post mortem might be done?" the DS asked.

"I'll be doing the preliminary PM this afternoon, and then, as you know, tissues will be sent to the lab for analysis and that will take anything from a few days to a few weeks, depending on what we're looking for, but you'll get my initial report later today, or first thing tomorrow. Cause of death seems clear enough but that too will be confirmed in due course."

Knowing that was all they would get for the time being, they thanked the pathologist and left him to do his work unhindered.

"I SUPPOSE it's time to speak to the lady who discovered the body," said Lottie, "I'm hoping that she might know more about who he is since, according to Tim, Dougie - that's the coastguard - thought he was a retired man who'd come to live on the island not long ago, although Dougie told him that he didn't actually know him."

"The lady's name is Mrs Jessie Grieves," Dean said, consulting his notebook and the coastguard gave me directions to her cottage. She was walking her dog when she found him."

"Poor woman!" Lottie remarked, "no doubt she'll be in a bit of a state but let's see what she can tell us."

"Yeah, and maybe there'll be a cup of tea in it, I didn't have time for breakfast." said the DC, his stomach rumbling noisily.

2

SANDHAM LANE

HOLY ISLAND

J ust as Dougie White had directed, the detectives found Mrs Grieves little cottage in the middle of Sandham Lane, just off Marygate, Holy Island's busiest thoroughfare.

During the summer and at low tide the streets below Lindisfarne Castle teemed with visitors, but at this early hour it was still relatively quiet with few day trippers about.

The cottage was whitewashed with a freshly painted green door and carefully tended flowers in hanging baskets on either side. DC Dean pressed the doorbell and there was the immediate response of Bertie's barking alerting his mistress that visitors had arrived. However, the old lady must have been looking out for them as the door was opened right away.

"Mrs Grieves?" asked Lottie, holding up her warrant card, "I'm Detective Sergeant Lockhart and this is Detective Constable Dean."

"Come in, come in," she said, hustling the friendly whippet ahead of her, "ye'll be ready for a cup of tea Ah expect. The kettle's on."

As they followed her up the narrow hall they could smell the mouth-watering aroma of fresh baking and Dean's stomach rumbled again.

Mrs Grieve led them into a sunny, south-facing kitchen-cum-living room which was deceptively roomy for such a small house. Modern double-glazed patio doors opened onto a view of the castle high on its promontory, with the expanse of sea beyond.

"Sit yourselves down," she said, switching on the kettle to come back to the boil, "Ah've just taken scones out of the oven, ye'll have some with yer tea?"

It was more a statement than a question, but Dean, without looking at Lottie for his cue, quickly replied, "Why, thanks Mrs Grieve, that would be champion."

"Ah hope ye don't mind dogs detectives," Mrs Grieve said, as Bertie was already sniffing the visitors with interest, "Ah can put him in another room if ye do."

Lottie, who was rubbing Bertie's velvety ears, replied, "I love dogs Mrs Grieves, especially sight hounds. I have a rescue greyhound which I see Bertie has already discovered. Bertie was closely examining every inch of Lottie's trouser legs, using his nose like a blind person reading braille with their fingers.

As Mrs Grieves chattered away, magpie-like, the officers drank the strong tea and ate the buttered scones. Lottie was happy to let her chatter on for a while, realising the older woman's stream of consciousness was her way of dealing with the shock she'd had earlier that morning.

Presently she looked at Dean who, understanding the tacit message, wiped the crumbs from his mouth and took out his notebook.

Lottie began by saying, "It must have been a terrible shock finding the body like that Mrs Grieves."

"Oh aye, it was awful," she shuddered as the image of the hanging man came back into her mind. "Ah think Ah'll be having' nightmares for a while."

"Do you know who he is?"

"Ah've seen him around although Ah don't know him to speak to ..." she paused, a little flustered, then corrected herself. "Ah mean Ah didn't know him to speak to. Ah think he's only been on the island for a few months." Bertie, who was a small dainty whippet, was now curled up on her lap and she was stroking his ears absently.

"Did you see anyone else around the Priory this morning?" Lottie asked.

"No, it's usually very quiet in the morning when the causeway's closed, otherwise there's always people and traffic coming from or going to the mainland for work. There are always the early dog walkers, of course, but nobody was near the Priory this morning."

Mrs Grieves went on to describe how she'd been contemplating the view when she'd heard Bertie whimpering, then her horrific discovery and her call to the emergency services.

Finally Lottie looked at Dean and they both stood up. "Thank you Mrs Grieves, you've been very helpful and thank you for the lovely tea and scones too, of course."

She handed her business card to the old lady and said, "If you remember anything else about this morning, no matter how trivial you think it is, please give me a call as it might help us with our investigation."

Mrs Grieves took the card and put Bertie onto an easy chair by the range and she saw the police officers to the door.

Lottie paused on the doorstep, turned around and, as an afterthought, asked "Do you have someone who could come and sit with you Mrs Grieves? You've had such a shock and today might be difficult for you."

"Aye, Ah do, Ah have a good friend in the village, Ah'll give her a call now. Thank you both, ye've been very kind."

"Bye Mrs Grieves," said Dean, "your scones were great, by the way. You take care now."

She watched them walk down the lane until they turned the corner into Marygate, then she went back into her cottage to phone her friend.

3

SUNDAY 17TH SEPTEMBER

Evening briefing

The Murder Investigation Team were gathered in the incident room at the police station in Berwick-upon-Tweed.

Although Northumbria MIT was based in Newcastle, major crimes in rural areas necessitated having a satellite base. This had the dual purpose of saving money and travelling time and, the advantage of having an ear on the ground as it were, meant that they would quickly pick up on local intelligence.

DS Lottie Lockhart stood by the whiteboard which had been filling up with the information collected and collated over the previous thirty-six hours, the crucial 'golden hour'.

At the top of the board was a photo of the deceased at the crime scene, alongside one of him alive. The room hummed with conversations in lowered tones when the DS spoke.

"Okay, the DI has obviously been held up on her way from Newcastle, so let's get started as there's a lot to get through."

The room fell silent and, pointing to the photo she said, "Right, what do we have so far? Seventy year old, recently retired priest, Fr Michael Donovan, was found hanging by the neck in the ruins of Lindisfarne Priory, on Holy Island, by an early morning dog walker."

"It's aye the poor dog walkers eh?" said the young Scotsman, PC Wright, a recent, enthusiastic addition to the team.

PC Gillian Wheatfield glared at him and he looked at his feet, suitably chastened. She'd been tasked with mentoring him and she looked apologetically towards the DS at this latest faux pas.

DS Lockhart continued, "He was identified through initial door to door enquiries by uniformed officers and SOCOs are at his home now as it's a potential crime scene and possibly the kill site."

At this point Detective Inspector Clelland slipped into the back of the room and motioned for Lockhart to continue. She wanted to see how her DS was handling the briefing and she was happy to let her get on with it for the time being.

"It was initially thought to be a suicide but the pathologist at the scene confirmed he'd been strangled before being strung up at the Priory.

Professor Healey's preliminary post mortem report, which he emailed to us first thing this morning, tells us that the victim was strangled using a polypropylene rope.

The small blue fibres found in the welt around the victim's neck are consistent with this type of rope and it's commonly used for a variety of functions including the mooring of boats, so it's probably very common on the island. There were no defensive wounds found on his body."

DI Clelland raised her hand and Lockhart asked, "Ma'm?"

"I suppose it's too early for the toxicology report to be back, but does the professor say anything about whether he'd been drinking?"

Lockhart looked at the printed email and replied, "Yes, there was a substantial amount of alcohol in his blood. Are you thinking that he may have been so intoxicated he was virtually unaware that he was being strangled?"

"It's possible," said the DI, "anything else that seems significant?"

"Yes Ma'am, two things," she said, checking her notes, "First thing: Professor Healey estimates the time of death at between 11 o'clock on Friday night and 1 o'clock on Saturday morning. Since the causeway was still open until 2.05 on Saturday morning, the perpetrator had sufficient time to remove the body to the Priory, hang him and then get off the island, that is if he left the island at all."

"And the second thing?" asked the DI.

"Paddy Healey's report remarks on the fact that there are early signs of Alzheimer's disease in the brain tissue, so that may also have been a factor in him not being able to defend himself."

"What lines of enquiry are you looking at so far?"

In response, Lockhart turned to DC Dean. "Gary, you've been looking into the priest's background, what do we know about him?"

Gary walked to the board and attached an A3 sheet with the parishes Fr Donovan had been placed in throughout his religious career.

"Fr Michael Donovan, ordained in Edinburgh in 1976,

was curate in four Edinburgh parishes before becoming Parish Priest in his last parish. As is the custom in the Catholic Church, a small property was provided for retirement and he chose to live on Holy Island."

"Did you get a sense of what kind of person he was Gary? I mean, someone obviously wanted him dead." Lottie asked.

"I'm still digging Sarge, but so far the opinion is that he was a nice guy, he'd been a well-known music teacher in his curate days, having taught many choir boys over the years."

"So, ye're thinkin' paedo right enough then?" PC Wright asked with excitement.

"Not all priests are paedophiles Jace!" retorted his mentor.

"Aye, but he had the word carved into his chest, for goodness sake!" the PC replied peevishly.

"Okay guys," admonished the DS without rancour, "we're not ruling anything out as a motive at this stage. Maybe the killer did that to put us on the wrong track." She turned back to Gary, her raised eyebrows asking the same question.

"So far, the intelligence is that Fr Donovan was a charismatic figure, said to be ..." he consulted his notebook, "very conscientious and offered extra tuition to the boys outside normal choir practice."

An excited murmur went round the room which Lockhart quelled, saying, "That may be innocent enough but it's a line of enquiry we definitely need to keep open. Don't rule others out because of it though."

She looked back at her DC and asked, "Anything else?"

"I need to talk to someone in the Diocesan Office but it's closed until tomorrow. I'll get onto them then."

"Good" Lockhart replied, "keep on with all that, see what surfaces."

"Boss." he nodded and sat down.

Turning to the lead CSI, she asked, "What do you have for us Tim?"

Tim Lightfoot, a shy man, stood up, cleared his throat and said, "Drag marks at the scene suggest the victim was dragged across the grass, so presumably killed elsewhere and moved to the Priory."

He continued, his voice now animated, "I also found clear boot prints and this might help in identifying the perpetrator." He walked to the board and added four large photographs.

"These shots show that the gait of the person is out of balance, suggesting one leg is shorter than the other, not by much but enough to cause this uneven gait. The cast taken shows he wore a size 11, probably an industrial type boot. I'll check the database for a brand when I get back to the lab and let you know."

"You're sure we're looking for a man Tim?" asked the DS.

"Without being sexist, I would say yes, or else a big and very strong woman to be able to move the dead weight, literally I mean, of a man the size of Fr Donovan and she would certainly stand out in a crowd." he replied, with a shy smile.

Thanks Tim, that's great work," said Lockhart, "and tomorrow's tasks while we await forensic results ..." she paused for effect, "please be aware that we have a window for safe crossing to and from the mainland between 08.55 and 15.30 so make the most of this time on the island. You've all been given sheets with the safe crossing times."

She looked around, making sure everyone had a copy as the last thing she needed was for any of the officers to need rescuing by the coastguards.

Knowing she had initially taken the briefing in DI Clelland's absence and not wanting to step on her senior officer's toes, she asked, "Would you like to take over now Ma'am?"

"Yes, thank you Lottie and my apologies to everyone for being late, there was an RTA on the A1 and the traffic was reduced to one lane." she said, as she walked up to the whiteboard.

"Right then," she said looking at the updated board, "you've made good progress so far, but we must push on. I want uniforms continuing with door to door enquiries, get CCTV footage if they have it on the island, or if any homes have cameras fitted. Did anyone hear or see anything?"

She turned to PCs Wheatfield and Wright, "Gillian, I want you and Jason to contact the priest's former parishes, find out what you can about the victim. Try to find where his ex-housekeepers are now, if they're still alive, and get as much background information on Fr Donovan as possible. We need to build up a picture of the man as well as the priest. Divide the parishes between you."

Dean looked at Lockhart in confusion as she had given him this task earlier in the briefing. Clelland turned to Lockhart and said, "I'm sorry to contradict your previous instructions to DC Dean."

She explained, "I think it would be a better use of time if you and Dean interview the priest's neighbours, I know you didn't have time yesterday because of the tides and then I want you to do a walkthrough of Fr Donovan's cottage and the Priory. The SOCOs will be out of the cottage by mid morning. Get a feel for the place and the man who lived there."

"Yes Ma'am" replied Lockhart, "will do."

"Okay, good work team," said the DI, "the next briefing

will be tomorrow evening at 6.30, let's hope we will know a lot more by then."

As chairs scraped back and the others left, Lockhart said to Dean, "Somebody must have seen or heard something, even if they don't realise it yet."

4

SUNDAY NIGHT

QUAYSIDE

Although it was a Sunday night the little restaurant was busy with people wanting to extend their weekend as long as possible. They were in Giovanni's on the Quayside in Berwick, which was a small family-run Italian restaurant and a favourite of Lottie's.

Lottie had finished a generous portion of penne funghi and had just waved away the offer of dessert, opting instead for a second glass of red wine. She smiled contentedly as she looked around her. The owners prided themselves on being able to provide their patrons with cosy, intimate tables at the back of the restaurant where they could converse without being overheard.

The only lighting in this area came from candles in wine bottles on the tables covered with red and white checked tablecloths and from the framed pictures of Italian scenes which were illuminated by little up-lighters.

After the waiter had brought her wine, Lottie looked at her companion and said, "Okay Frank, I can tell there's something on your mind, so are you going to tell me what's bothering you?" She smiled at him fondly and put her hand on his, inviting him to speak and tell her what was wrong.

Frank took both her hands in his and gently squeezed them. In his strong Geordie accent, he said, "Well Pet, it's just that we've been datin' for eighteen months like, an' Ah'm wonderin' where our relationship is goin'?"

Lottie thought, "Not this again!" But with a smile to take any hurt from her words, she said instead, "It's still early days Frank and we've been through all this before. You know I don't want to rush into anything, not after … not after what happened in my last relationship."

He looked crestfallen and she added gently, "I thought you understood that sweetheart?" It was more a question than a statement of fact.

"Ah know Pet, Ah do know how badly tret you were, but surely you know me by now? Ah'm not like that psychopath ye were married to, Ah'd never hurt ye. Ah love ye Lottie."

Lottie looked at him for a long moment and he wondered what was in that look - was it pity or sadness? Eventually she said, "I know you do Frank and I love you too as a lover and a friend, but I'm just not ready to commit to anything long term, not yet anyway. Besides," she said after a pause, "you're still healing from the pain of those awful years with your ex-wife, surely you want to take things slowly too?"

Frank had been two years out of a very acrimonious divorce when they'd met at a conference on coercive control and domestic abuse, a multi-disciplinary event in Newcastle, some eighteen months previously.

Frank worked as a psychotherapist in various NHS settings and had been seeing increasing numbers of women who were in abusive relationships and who were struggling to leave violent partners.

Lottie had been there on behalf of Northumbria Police who had recently launched an initiative with officers specially trained in liaising with women's refuges, to offer information and advice to the women there.

Frank and Lottie had 'clicked' right away during the morning break on the first day, discovering that they had a lot in common. They'd started dating then, seeing each other just once a week, then more frequently, making meals for each other and spending some weekends together, when Lottie's shifts allowed.

"What is it that's keeping you from making a commitment Lottie? Ah'm tryin' really hard to understand Pet. Ah mean, we get on great together, a perfect match on many levels, especially in the bedroom. Ah just can't see what the problem is." He shook his head, his big, puppy-like, eyes sad.

She thought about the question she'd grappled with so many times over the past few months since Frank first suggested they live together. Lately though, it had begun to feel like pressure.

She'd had many a one-sided conversation with Dolly along the following lines: "What *is* stopping me Dolly? He's a lovely man, very considerate, gentle and you adore him, so what am I afraid of?" Dolly would just cock her head from one side to the other, as though she was considering her mistress's questions, ears standing out at right angles from her head.

Lottie would continue, "Is it fear of losing my hard-won independence and freedom? Or am I afraid of falling into the same trap that I did with *him*?" She rarely spoke his name since escaping from Denis McIvor fifteen years earlier. But she said none of this to Frank who was regarding her and waiting for an answer.

"Why don't we leave things as they are for a little while longer, eh love? See how we go?" She hated herself at that moment, as she saw the naked disappointment on his face.

He sighed and said, "A'right Pet," then added, shaking his head sadly, "but Ah can't wait for ever Lottie, that wouldn't be fair."

Lottie nodded her understanding. "Fair enough love, how about leaving it for three months eh? Make a decision by Christmas?"

By tacit agreement they left the subject there, both of them feeling a degree of compromise had been made: Lottie had negotiated more time to think about their relationship and Frank had a deadline by which he would have his answer.

Suddenly Lottie yawned. "I really should be getting home Frank, I've got an early start tomorrow and you know how busy it gets in the early days of an investigation."

"Aye Pet, Ah know." Frank stood up and helped her on with her jacket. "Come on then, let's get you home, Dolly will be waiting for you." He smiled at her, his good humour restored.

5

ST CUTHBERT'S SQUARE, HOLY ISLAND

Monday 18th September

Lockhart and Dean sat in the small tidy sitting room in the cottage next door to where Fr Donovan had lived for the past few months, talking to Mr and Mrs Smith, a typical old Northumbrian couple. The neighbours on the other side of the priest's cottage were away for a long weekend and hadn't yet returned.

Mrs Smith, a spritely eighty year old, had just poured tea for the detectives and she placed a large plate of fruit cake in front of them.

"Help yersel Pet," she encouraged, pushing the plate closer.

"Thank you Mrs Smith," said Dean enthusiastically, "that looks delicious."

Lottie groaned inwardly and thought, "I'll be two stones heavier by the time this murder is solved." But she said, "Thank you." and chose the smallest piece she could find.

"A terrible business!" exclaimed Mr Smith, from his chair by the fireside. He'd been sitting reading when the police arrived and had placed his book face down on his lap, his reading glasses hanging around his neck by a cord.

"Aye, Michael was such a nice chap, an awful thing to happen to him, so it is," agreed his wife.

"Did either of you see anyone going into the priest's house on Friday night?" Lottie asked.

"No," replied Mrs Smith, "it's dark by eight o'clock these nights so the curtains would be closed."

"What about you Mr Smith?" Dean had finished eating and was taking notes.

"Ah was in the Ship Inn from about half past seven until ten o'clock," he said, "Ah always meet my pal for a pint on Friday nights."

"Did either of you hear anything? Arguing or a commotion next door?" asked Lottie, "What about later on when you came back from the pub Mr Smith?"

"Ah didn't hear anything like that, but Ah'm a bit deaf," he looked at his wife, "what about you Peggy?"

Peggy shook her head. "No, but then Ah'm a wee bit deaf too and the telly's on quite loud."

"Did Michael get a lot of visitors?" Lottie then asked.

"There were some when he first moved in, but not many lately," Mrs Smith said. "He was a man who seemed to be happy with his own company but he was always pleasant when ye met him in the street or if he was in the garden when Ah was hanging out the washin'," she reflected. "And we'd sometimes hear him playin' the piano - he was a lovely pianist, you know, classical stuff like, but it was lovely all the same." She looked at her husband for confirmation.

"That's right, Ah'd see him out walkin' around the island, sometimes up by Gertrude Jekyll's garden or heading towards the dunes, usually when the tide was in," he said, "there are fewer people about then, ye know," he added by way of explanation.

"Ah would take him in some scones and cake on my baking days," Mrs Smith said, "but he never invited me in, just thanked me. Ah think he was reserved, as they say."

Lottie and Dean exchanged glances and, knowing they weren't going to get much more useful information from the couple, Lottie stood up and said, "Thank you Mr and Mrs Smith, you've been very helpful." She handed them her card and added, "Please give us a call if you remember anything else."

Dean was putting his notebook into his pocket when Mr Smith said, "There was a car parked in front of Michael's house when Ah came home from the pub, Ah remember thinkin' that Ah hadn't seen it before. Ah've just remembered."

"Do you know what the make of the car was Mr Smith?"

He shook his head, "No, sorry, Ah'm not up on the cars nowadays, there's that many different kinds, not like in my day."

"Is there anything at all that you remember about it?" asked Dean, retrieving his notebook from his pocket.

"All Ah can tell ye is that it was one o' them great big things, silver Ah think but it was hard to tell in the dark wi' just the lights from the cottages to see by."

"Do you mean like a 4x4 Mr Smith?" Lottie asked.

"Aye, could've been something like that," he replied and added, "a big ugly square shaped bugger."

"Well thanks anyway Mr Smith and if you do think of anything else ..."

"Aye hinny," Peggy said, holding up the card Lottie had given her, "we've got yer number."

6

ST CUTHBERT'S COTTAGE
A SHORT TIME LATER

There was a new-looking name plaque on the wall, next to the front door. It was oval-shaped bearing a gold coloured cross with the words *St Cuthbert's Cottage* underneath. Lockhart and Dean showed their warrant cards to the uniformed officer guarding the door to the priest's house.

"Ma'am," he said and he opened the door to let them in, "Mr Lightfoot is waiting for you inside."

Tim had arranged to meet them there to walk and talk them through, what they now knew, was the scene of the murder. The SOCOs had finished collecting evidence but the footplates and forensic markers were still in place.

A small hallway led into the living room where a cluster of markers were situated around an armchair at one side of the fireplace.

"What can you tell us Tim?" Lottie asked, looking around the comfortably furnished room.

There was a cottage-style sofa in a floral fabric with its matching chair by the side of the wood burning stove. The mantlepiece had some ornaments and silver framed photographs of Fr Donovan in various settings, usually at what appeared to be church events.

On the floor, in front of the hearth, lay a large framed photo of the priest with a group of choir boys. It had obviously been taken by a professional photographer and the glass had been smashed into so many little pieces that they sparkled incongruously in the autumn sunshine that came through the south facing window.

Lottie pointed to it and asked, "May I take this Tim?"

"Yes, of course, everything has been dusted for finger prints. Let me remove it from the frame for you first."

He handed her the photo and she and Gary peered at it closely.

"He looks to be in his mid thirties in this photo," she said, "and the boys faces are quite clear which should help us in identifying them."

She turned the photo over and looked at the back. As she thought, the inscription read, *St Andrew's Church Choir, June 1986"* and the photographer's stamp *Peter Markham Photographers, Edinburgh*.

"As you can see from the space on the mantlepiece Boss, it obviously had pride of place in the middle."

"So it probably had sentimental value for the priest," she said.

"And it looks like an object of the killer's hatred, given how smashed up the frame is," remarked Dean.

"I wonder if one of these boys is the man we're now looking for?" Lottie mused.

The piano which Peggy Smith had mentioned, was positioned against one wall and when Lottie got closer to it, she could see that the polished wood was scored with cuts and gouges. She looked at Tim, eyebrows raised.

"Looks like it was done with a screwdriver, although we

didn't find one lying around," he said in response, "the piano was obviously another object that the perpetrator detested."

"We know there were no defensive wounds Tim, but was there any sign of a struggle?" Lottie asked.

"None," replied Tim, but judging by the table here," he indicated a table next to the armchair where an almost empty whisky bottle and glass sat, "he may well have been quite drunk, although there's no way of telling how much was in the bottle to start with. We've taken fingerprints from it which don't belong to the victim and which aren't on our data base but which match those on the doorbell, so the killer may well have been systematically feeding him the alcohol over a period of a couple of hours."

"That's very possible," agreed Dean, "and the PM report states that he had a substantial amount of alcohol in his system."

"There are no signs of a forced entry which means the priest let the murderer into his home," added Tim.

"So, someone he knew and who he had no reason to fear," Lottie said, looking around the room again.

"Are we done here Sarge?" Dean asked.

"Yes Gary, we've seen what we need to, let's do a final walkthrough at the Priory and then we'll get back to base."

The Priory

THE BLUE AND white police tape around the inner cordon of the ancient ruins of Lindisfarne Priory flapped in the wind as they approached and the uniformed officer logged their details as they entered. The site would remain closed until the SOCOs were sure they had all the evidence they could possibly lift from the scene.

Lottie was standing deep in thought when Gary said, "Penny for them Sarge."

Coming out of her reverie she said, "Oh I was just thinking of the incongruity of it all." She moved her arms in a sweeping motion, taking in the ancient ruins of the Priory and the view which encompassed Lindisfarne Castle, on its promontory and the Northumberland coast all the way down to Bamburgh.

Dean looked around to where she was indicating and a little puzzled, he asked, "How do you mean exactly Sarge?"

"Well," she replied slowly, searching for the words to best express what she meant. "This is such a spiritual place. Pilgrims have been making their way from all over for centuries and people still believe that St Cuthbert's healing energy remains here to this day. It's not called Holy Island for nothing."

"Yes, I see what you mean," Dean replied, then added, "while today's pilgrims are mainly tourists who flock to the island in their hundreds at low tide, visiting the castle or to go bird and seal watching on the nature reserve."

Lottie sighed deeply and said, "You know, I can't help thinking that the killer chose this spot deliberately. He went to all the trouble of getting the body out of the cottage, unseen, transporting it here and hanging him when it would have been easier, and less risky, to string him up in his cottage."

"So, what are you saying Sarge?"

"Okay, for the sake of argument, let's go with the theory that the motive for killing the priest was revenge for being sexually abused by him in the past," she began, "I think that the killer is making a point about peadophile priests and the hypocrisy of the Catholic Church, and how it has repeatedly turned a blind eye to what's been going on for decades and, even worse, the way it has protected priests from prosecution by dealing with any reports and complaints in-house, as it were."

"Yes, I do see that, although it is still only one line of enquiry at the moment," Dean said.

"Yeah, I know Gary, but it does lend strength to the theory and I can't help thinking that he chose this place as a gesture, you know to despoil it - like a sacrilege - as if he was getting revenge for being robbed of his innocence at a young age, when priests were up on pedestals as 'men of God'. At the same time, a great number of them were using their position of trust to abuse children, probably still are."

Lottie, who knew she was like a dog with a bone when focused on an investigation, suddenly stopped talking and laughed.

"Care to share the joke Sarge?" asked Dean, smiling along with her.

"Oh, it's just me getting carried away and seeing this," once more gesturing around the Priory grounds, "as the murderer's way of giving his middle finger to the Catholic Church and its sanctimonious trappings."

"Well, I would say that could be a pretty strong motive for murder right enough," Dean agreed.

Outside the police cordon, curious onlookers peered in at the scene of the gruesome discovery, ice creams in hand, as though this was just another tourist attraction. Murder, it seemed, especially the murder of a stranger, was always fascinating.

TEAM BRIEFING

Monday 18th September, 6pm

The incident room in Berwick police station was a hive of activity now, with officers co-opted as reader-receivers of information coming in from the public.

DCI Flynn, at HQ in Newcastle, was the SIO (Senior Investigating Officer) who was project managing this, along with other on-going serious crime investigations.

He had given a brief statement to the media the previous evening and had appealed for any witnesses to come forward by contacting the helpline number. By Monday the national and local papers carried the story along with their online counterparts and the volume of calls and emails was building up.

DI Clelland had left a big box of Danish pastries in the incident room earlier for the team and they were just finishing the unexpected treat when she entered the room to begin the evening briefing.

The team fell silent as she stood in front of the whiteboards. Another had been brought in to accommodate the new information that was coming in all the time.

"As you can see, the SIO has named this investigation 'Operation Seagull' and by the look of these boards, you've all been very busy." She turned to Lockhart and Dean.

"Did you get anything useful from the neighbours DS Lockhart?" she asked.

Lottie stood up, "Ma'am, the neighbours on one side have been on holiday, so nothing there," she said, "but the old couple who live on the other side told us that Michael Donovan was a quiet man who kept himself to himself. He didn't get many visitors after the initial few when he first moved into the cottage, but he was always polite when he saw the Smiths on the street or in the garden."

"Okay," said Clelland, "get uniforms to go when the absent neighbours return, see if they were aware of anything suspicious in the days before they went away."

"Ma'am. The neighbours who live further along reported nothing unusual or suspicious to the uniforms making door to door enquiries. The old man, Mr Smith, said that when he got back from his local at ..." She looked at Dean who had been who had been taking notes during the interview.

"Yes Boss," Dean said, rifling through his notebook to the relevant page, "Mr Smith said he'd been in the Ship Inn with his friend and got back around ten o'clock."

"Thanks Gary," said Lottie, "Mr Smith said that there was a car parked outside the priest's house that he didn't recognise and which hadn't been there when he left for the pub at seven-thirty. He didn't think to take a note of the registration number and he didn't know the make or model of the car."

Clelland was beginning to lose patience and she asked, "Did you get any useful information from this old couple?"

"Yes Ma'am, sorry, I was just coming to that," Lottie replied reddening from the mild rebuke. "While the old man couldn't say what make of car it was, his description matches that of some 4x4's."

The DI nodded and addressed the PCs. "PC's Wheatfield and Wright I want you to follow that up on ANPR footage from the A1 in both directions - north and southbound - after the causeway opened at ..." she checked the board for the tide times" 02.05 onwards. The A1 won't have been so busy then, so you may get lucky."

"Yes Ma'am," PC Wright answered for them both, with his perpetual enthusiasm.

"Also check the footage from before the causeway closed," Clelland consulted the tide timetable again, "at 13.55 on the Friday afternoon." Wheatfield and Wright nodded and noted it down.

She looked at the sheaf of papers she'd been given by the officers taking information to the public and frowned. "As usual when an appeal has been made to the public, we have been inundated with calls and emails and, as usual, there will probably be a fair number of crank calls, but we must follow up on all reasonable information." She turned to Tim Lightfoot next.

"Tim, you've now finished in the priest's home, what can you tell us?"

"Boss," he said and stood up. "The report from the pathologist on the alcohol consumed ties up with the almost empty bottle of whisky on the table by the armchair we now know the priest was sitting on when he was strangled. Minute fibres from the rope used to strangle him were found in the fabric of the chair. There were no signs of him having put up any resistance - nothing was knocked over or upset which you'd expect if he'd struggled or put up a fight." Clelland nodded and he continued.

"Certain items in the room had been badly damaged suggesting the depth of rage that the killer felt towards the victim, but it wasn't indiscriminate. I mean they were things to do with the priest, you know, to do with what he was and what he did, I think ..." he trailed off, unsure of how to phrase what he was trying to say.

"Go on," said the DI.

"We know that he was musical and had taught choir boys, so it seems significant that his piano was vandalised and a photo frame containing that photo of him with some of the boys," he pointed to the group photo that Lottie had added to the board before the meeting.

"It's as though he destroyed the things that he knew were precious to the victim or those that had been significant in his role as choir master."

"I see," said Clelland, inspecting the photo closely, "I wonder if one of these little boys is our murderer," echoing what Lottie had wondered earlier.

"I wonder why he didn't rip it up or burn it?" asked PC Wright, leaning forward to peer at the photo.

"It's a starting point anyway," replied the DI, "send a copy of it to all of his former parishes, try to get an ID for each of those boys." She turned back to Tim, realising she'd wandered off from the forensic report. "Do you have anything else for us Tim?"

"Two more things Ma'am, at the moment. Firstly we lifted fingerprints from the doorbell and the whisky bottle which don't match the priest's and which are not on the

PNC, so if they belong to our killer, he has no previous," he said, then continued, "The second thing is the bootprints were made by Caterpillar, they're a make of waterproof safety boots, the kind worn by workers in the construction industry."

"Thanks Tim, we'll bear that in mind once we have actual suspects in our midst," replied Clelland.

"Okay where are we now?" she asked, appraising the murder boards. "We have a probable motive - possible past sexual abuse of boys in his care - but the word *paedophile* that was carved into his chest could equally be a false clue to throw us off," she said, literally getting into her stride, as she paced back and forth, occasionally stopping in front of the boards.

Denise Clelland was a career police officer in her early thirties who had joined the police service as a graduate entrant at the level of Detective Inspector. She was well liked for her fairness, although she spoke her mind and didn't suffer fools gladly. Her colleagues 'upstairs' expected her to reach the higher ranks, perhaps as far as ACC before retirement. She didn't want her excellent crime solving record to flounder on this seemingly messy investigation.

"If revenge is the motive for the priest's murder, we have a number of unknown-as-yet suspects who need, as a matter of urgency to be TIE'd and that is no small job." (TIE is police shorthand for "traced, interviewd and eliminated")

She stopped her pacing, took a deep breath and said, "I want you, PCs Wright and Wheatfield, to get onto the Edinburgh parishes, first thing tomorrow, for as much information as possible regarding choir boys around this time." she pointed to the photo on the board again.

"Boss," they both replied at the same time.

"Gary, did you manage to contact the Diocesan Office in Edinburgh today?" she asked.

"Yes Ma'am," he replied, " I got on to them this afternoon after interviewing the Smiths."

"And?"

"And the person I spoke to tried to fob me off on various admin staff and when I finally got through to someone in authority - a Fr Francis Logan - I was told that Fr Donovan's personnel record is confidential and he was more interested in finding out when his body would be released as he had a funeral to arrange."

"So, at best he was unhelpful?" asked Clelland, "Did you get a sense that he was trying to hide something?"

"Yes, I would say he was. He got quite rattled when I said we needed to see the priest's personal file and when I emphasised that this was a murder enquiry, he changed the subject to the funeral arrangements."

She thought about this for a few moments then said, "Okay, let's see what we can dig up from the parishes first and, if necessary, we'll get a warrant to access those records further down the road."

"Yes Boss," said Dean, nodding agreement.

"I'll be in Newcastle tomorrow, giving evidence at a trial, so I want you, DS Lockhart, to take charge of the day-to-day running of the case. Call me if you need me or, if it's urgent and I'm in court, speak to DCI Flynn."

"Yes Ma'am."

"You all know what you've to do in the meantime and I'll be back here on Wednesday. DCI Flynn is meeting the press this evening and he'll be using a copy of this photo," she pointed to the board behind her, "asking for the men who were the boys in this photo to contact us. So you may find yourselves run off your feet over the next few days doing follow up interviews. We'll get extra bodies from Newcastle if necessary but do as much as possible by phone. Any questions?"

PC Wheatfield raised her hand, "Gillian?" Clelland asked.

"Ma'am, I was just wondering whether PC Wright and I might be more effective if we went to the Edinburgh parishes in person to search the parish records and bring copies back."

After just a few seconds pause the DI said, "That's a good point Gillian and it's sometimes harder to refuse requests in person than on the phone. Yes, do that and I'll clear the expenses for it with the DCI."

PC Wright was almost beside himself with excitement at the thought of actually going to Edinburgh and working like a 'real detective', as he thought of it. Then, with a severe look from his mentor, he sobered up.

"On second thoughts," Clelland spoke again, " PCs Wheatfield and Wright, forget what I said about splitting the parishes between you, that would have worked if you were phoning them. Go together in one car and save on expense."

Then, after another pause, she said, "In which case, Lockhart and Dean, you take over the ANPR job that the PCs were going to do."

She then added, "Look, I'm sorry if you feel you've been messed about with the change in tasks, it's just me thinking on my feet." (ANPR stands for "automatic number plate recognition")

"No worries Ma'am," Lottie reassured her.

"Any more questions before we go home?" the DI asked.

"No Ma'am," replied Lottie, "but may I thank you on

behalf of the team for the delicious pastries. They hit the spot and will keep me going until I get my supper."

"You're welcome team. Now get home and get some rest." she concluded the meeting, gathering her things to leave.

8

MONDAY 18TH SEPTEMBER

Later that night

The mist from the river had risen and was swirling in patches around the ruins of Norham Castle, so that parts of the castle appeared to move eerily in and out of view.

Lottie shivered, not from cold as it was unusually mild for the time of year and that late at night. But a feeling of unease had crept over her as she walked with Dolly up the steep brae to the castle. She felt as though she was being watched.

She turned around but the silent street was empty, there wasn't even a car passing through the village. She shook her head and laughed mirthlessly, trying to shake off the silly notion and the strange feeling.

"Time to go home Dolly," she said as they approached the castle gate and they turned quickly to walk back down the hill to the main street and her cottage.

As she picked up her pace, she was sure she could hear the faint padding of footsteps some way behind. She stopped and turned round to look but there was no one there and the sound of footsteps had ceased. There was only the empty street in a village that was always deserted at this time of night.

She'd been later than usual leaving work and the two pubs in the village had long since closed and no late night revellers lingered on the street. She now wished she'd taken the DI's advice and gone home when the others had left, but she had wanted to prepare for the next day's work at such a crucial stage in the investigation and, especially, when she had been put in charge.

Just as they reached the front door of her cottage Dolly froze and looked back along the way they had come, her hackles rose and a low growl emanated from her. Without looking back, Lottie unlocked the door and hurriedly led Dolly inside. She quickly locked the door, secured the bolts and deftly unclipped the lead from Dolly's collar.

Keeping the lights switched off, she felt her way to the living room and crept to the window and looked out onto the street. She watched as a dark figure slipped into a car which was parked further down the street. It was parked away from the street lighting so it was in a pool of darkness between lamp posts. After some moments it moved slowly through the village and she lost sight of it.

Lottie let out the breath she'd been holding, switched on the lamps and closed the curtains, making sure the window was locked. She sat slowly down on the sofa and patted Dolly's head, trying to soothe her canine companion who was clearly distressed at her mistress's fear. She placed her head on Lottie's knee and whimpered softly, in solidarity with her mistress.

Still feeling stunned, Lottie gave herself a mental shake and, in her usual self-composed voice, she said to the hound, "Come on Dolly, let's get you some milk and biscuits before bedtime."

At the mention of the treat, her ears picked up and her tail wagged happily in anticipation of her bedtime snack. While Dolly munched her treat Lottie poured herself a small brandy and sat down to consider what had happened and what had disturbed them both so much.

This wasn't the first time she'd been followed in the past week. On at least two previous occasions she was sure that she was being tracked, and had a strong feeling that she was being watched. And tonight, well, she actually heard footsteps behind her and she saw the dark figure walking furtively to the car that she was sure had been deliberately parked in the shadows.

Dolly was snuggled beside her on the sofa now and she sipped the comforting, amber liquid that warmed the chill that had entered her heart. As she rubbed the dog's velvety ears she thought aloud, "Who's been following us Dolly? And does it have anything to do with work?"

Dolly, like most dogs, was a good listener but that's as far as it went, and in response, she gave a big sigh and settled her head between her paws.

"So no help from you, as usual," Lottie smiled at her precious girl and she tried to make sense of these recent, and unsettling, events.

Having worked with Northumbria Police for more than a decade she'd helped to put away her share of criminals, some of them murderers, but none stood out as a threat now and none had just been released from prison.

She bemoaned the fact that Norham did not have any CCTV cameras in the village, although it was a good thing

in a way, since it meant that the village was deemed safe and
secure enough not to need them ... "until now maybe ..." she
thought aloud.

"Oh well," she told Dolly, "I shall just have to be more
vigilant and aware of what's going on around me when I'm
out and about."

Then doubts crept into her mind and she wondered if
her imagination was running away with her. A hot flush
crept up her back from the base of her spine making her
hair and face clammy and uncomfortable. "Damn!" she
thought, "if these symptoms continue I'm going to have to
see the doctor - if I ever find time to do that."

She fanned her face with her hand in a futile effort to
cool down and finished the last few drops of the brandy.
She'd just laid laid the glass on the side table when a
chilling thought struck her. "Whoever that was tonight," she
said to the sleeping dog, "he knows where I live." But something about that retreating figure was niggling away at the
back of her mind, there was something familiar, yet distant,
about it.

She sat brooding for a long time before rousing herself
and said, "Come on Dolly, it's time for bed, but will I sleep?"
she wondered.

Dolly got up slowly, shook her large, sleek body and
followed Lottie into the bedroom where she would sleep on
the king size bed, guarding her mistress.

9

DETECTIVE CONSTABLE GARY DEAN

While Lottie pondered over her stalker, Gary Dean lay on his bed, paralysed by the images and the voice in his mind. The nightmares and flashbacks had started again after years of being bliss-fully free of them.

"Come on now Gary, you know you want to play our little game." The old man was holding the boy's fingers firmly around the erection beneath his cassock. The vestry was empty, the other altar boys had scarpered away quickly so they wouldn't be left alone with the priest and his depraved appetite.

The cloying small of incense clung to his nostrils, making it hard for him to breathe. Terror took hold of him and he felt frozen to the spot, literally petrified. The priest had him trapped between the upright wooden chair he was sitting on and the table used to hold the vestments for mass.

The old man had removed his stole, apparently even he thought it a step too far to take his pleasure whilst still wearing the most holy of all vestments. The priest was breathing raggedly now, the stench from his breath making Gary feel sick and he wanted to retch. The priest had tightened the boy's grip around his hardness and he began to grope the area between the boy's legs.

"*NO!*" He screamed himself awake and was aware that he was back in the present, safe in his flat in Morpeth, sweating and struggling to breathe. His heart raced so fast he felt like he had just crossed the finishing line of the Great North Run.

He swung his legs round and sat hunched on the side of the bed, trying to get his breathing under control, his mind still jammed with contradictory thoughts and feelings: images of his wedding day and the guilty, shameful feelings from his past; his ten year old twin daughters and his passionate desire to keep them safe from the horrors he had experienced in childhood; and finally, anger, sadness and frustration that he was prevented from doing this since his wife had told him she wanted him out of the family home twelve months earlier.

She'd told him she couldn't live with his bouts of depression any more, even though he'd promised to see a couple's therapist to work through their marital difficulties. He remembered her cruel words, "It's not me that has the fucking problem Gary, so why should I see a counsellor?"

She was a primary school teacher and he suspected that she was having an affair with one of her colleagues, a man called Joules Arnott. She had started wearing smart clothes and makeup to work, something she'd not done in all their time together. Then there was the increasing number of after work meetings she said she had to attend and the girls were being left with her mother to look after more and more often.

He sighed deeply and shook his head in an attempt to clear the jumble of thoughts, then he went into the cramped kitchen to put the kettle on. As he sat at the kitchen table waiting for the kettle to boil he looked around the room, a great sadness flooding through him.

After almost twenty years service in the police and coming up to his fortieth birthday he thought, "Is this all I've got to show for my life?" After paying a generous sum in maintenance for his daughters and agreeing to them remaining in the comfortable three bedroomed family home in Gosforth, an affluent suburb of Newcastle, it didn't leave much for him to live on.

He hadn't been able to afford to rent in Newcastle, so he'd found a small flat in Morpeth, above the Oxfam charity shop on the main street, even though it meant a thirty minute daily commute to Northumbria Police HQ in Wallsend.

"It's best the girls lives aren't disrupted any more than necessary," Shirley had said, rationalising her demand that he move out and they stayed where they had lived, content-edly, as he'd believed, for the past ten years.

The furnished flat suited him at the time since Shirley had made it clear that she would not part with any of the household goods they'd bought jointly for the family home, citing the children's comfort and stability as a reason. However, he knew now from the acrimonious divorce process, that she was greedy and vindictive and did not want him to get his fair and legal share of their accrued assets from their life together as a couple.

When they'd first separated, she had feigned compro-mise over the joint belongings and access to the twins, but it didn't take him long to realise that he would have to fight tooth and nail for anything he was going to get from the divorce, including time with his beloved daughters.

When the nearby church struck two o'clock he got up from the table, rinsed his mug and left it to drain on the side of the sink. He had to be up at the crack of dawn if he was to drive to Berwick and be in the office by 8am. He only hoped that he would be able to sleep after the disturbing dream and the awful memories.

"Damn you Fr Michael Donovan for getting yourself murdered on our patch! Fuckin' pervert priests," he said to the empty room, but they were words of tired resignation rather than rage. He knew that he would have to pick himself up again tomorrow if he was to be able to effectively contribute to the investigation.

10

TUESDAY 19TH SEPTEMBER

Berwick Incident Room

Lottie was already at her desk when Dean arrived carrying two takeaway coffees. She looked up as he entered the room and noticed the dark circles under his eyes.

"Morning Gary," she greeted him, trying to sound brighter than she felt, as he laid one of the coffees in front of her. The aroma of the freshly ground coffee made her mouth water. "Mmm, that smells divine, thank you, and just what I need this morning. I had a bit of a disturbed night."

He peered at her closely and saw how tired she looked too. "Anything wrong?" he asked, concerned.

"Nah!," she waved her hand dismissing his worried look, "it's just the usual, during the early stages of an investigation." She wasn't going to tell anyone about her thinking she was being followed in case they thought she was just a paranoid, menopausal woman.

Instead she said," "What about you? You're looking a bit dark under the eyes - not your usual bright-eyed and bushy-tailed self," she added to lighten the enquiry.

"Same," he said, taking off his jacket and sitting down at his desk. He switched on his computer and looked around the room, which was empty except for the officers handling calls and emails from the public. Since last night's press conference and appeal, a number of people reported being or, knowing, at least one of the people in the group photo.

"Have Gillian and Jason left for Edinburgh already?" he asked.

"Yes, Gillian was collecting Jason from the front door, he was a little miffed that Gillian was to be the driver." she chuckled.

"Yes," agreed Dean smiling, "he would be, his visions of driving in a high speed chase up the A1 would be crushed."

"And speaking of the A1 Gary, we'd best get started on the ANPR footage," she said, "shouldn't take us long if we keep our heads down."

"I suppose so Sarge," said Dean, whose eyes were already tired and feeling gritty from the lack of sleep, and he was not relishing the task.

The A1 north had been fairly quiet on the night in question and, after just fifteen minutes looking at the footage, Dean cried, "Got it Sarge!"

Lottie paused the video she was studying and went over to Dean's desk to look at the screen. They could see what looked like a silver coloured 4x4 vehicle. Gary froze the video and a Toyota Land Cruiser had been captured clearly by the camera on the A1 northbound by the Haggerston junction at 02.00 on the Saturday morning.

"Zoom in Gary, so we can see the registration plate," Lottie instructed.

"Shit!" Gary said, "it's only a partial. Looks like the rest of it is caked in mud."

"Write down what we can see," Lottie said.

"SK08 is all I can get," he replied, frustrated.

"Okay, let's work with that. I think that's an Edinburgh registration, so that narrows it down and it also fits in with where Donovan was a priest all those years. I'd say we have a solid connection now," she said, optimism sounding in her voice, for the first time that day. "Find out how many Toyota Land Cruisers were registered in Edinburgh in 2008."

"Boss," Gary said, picking up on Lottie's mood, "I'll get onto that now."

"No point in me looking at the southbound footage, so I'll try to locate when he came onto the island which will be more of a needle in a haystack job, since the causeway was open for a while during the day," she said turning to consult the large tide crossing timetable on the murder board. "He cut it fine leaving the island if he had reached Haggerston at two o'clock."

"Yeah, maybe getting the priest to the Priory and strung up took him longer than he'd anticipated," Dean mused.

"Or smashing the photo and vandalising the piano," added Lottie.

Just then the internal phone rang and Lottie picked it up. It was one of the officers taking calls from the public. "Okay, put him through," she said.

"Good morning Sir, you're speaking to Detective Sergeant Lockhart." As Lottie spoke to the caller, Dean listened to her end of the conversation.

"Alright Sir, we'll meet you in your office at eleven-thirty tomorrow. Thank you for your call Dr McGuire," she said and hung up.

Dean was looking at her expectantly as she sighed, puffing out her cheeks.

"Well that was interesting!"

"A lead?" Dean asked feeling hopeful for the first time since the investigation began.

"Maybe," she said thoughtfully.

"Are you going to tell me or do I have to go down on my knees and beg?" Dean teased.

"Dr John McGuire says he is a lecturer in the Department of Social Policy at Edinburgh University," Lottie told him, "and he said he might know who killed the priest but he didn't want to speak about it on the phone."

"Do you think he's genuine or a crank?"

"He sounded genuine enough," Lottie replied, typing on her keyboard, "yes, here he is." She swivelled the screen round so Dean could see. "It says, 'John McGuire: MA Honours in Social Policy; Ph.D; Lecturer in the History of the Welfare State and Social Work Practice.'"

She sat back, drumming her fingers on the table. "We might just have the lead we've been looking for, but I'm not going to get too optimistic. We have an appointment with him tomorrow morning at the university."

"Let's see what he has to say then, and in the meantime, I'll try to track down this Toyota Land Cruiser," said Dean.

Lottie went back to the tedious task of trying to ascertain when the vehicle had arrived on the island earlier on the Friday.

At one o'clock Lottie logged off her computer and rubbed her tired eyes. "If I don't have a break I'm going to be cross-eyed looking at this grainy black and white footage."

Dean looked up and smiled, "Yeah, it's a right strain on the eyes Sarge, I just got lucky landing the north bound traffic."

"I didn't have time to prepare lunch this morning so I'm going to Greggs for a cheese and onion stottie, do you want anything?" Lottie usually brought a healthy lunch with her but because of her disturbed night she'd overslept and just had time to take Dolly for a short walk before getting ready for work.

"Yeah, same for me please," said Dean, handing her a five pound note.

"Do you want a drink to go with it?"

He was about to say yes when he remembered his straitened circumstances and the coffees he'd bought for them that morning, so he decided against the luxury. "Nah, Ah'll just make a cup of tea here," he replied, pointing to the kettle in the corner, on the tray with tea bags etc.

"Okay, I won't be long," she picked up her jacket and bag and left the room.

THEY CHATTED about the case while they ate lunch and when Dean asked, "So, what do you think Dr McGuire can tell us?"

Lottie seemed not to have heard him as she was staring into space.

"Sarge?" he said.

She realised he must have been talking and she hadn't heard a word he'd said. "Sorry Gary, I was miles away, what did you say?"

Dean repeated the question.

"I honestly don't know but he seemed agitated, as though he wanted to get something off his chest."

"And what about you?" Dean asked.

"I'm sorry, I don't understand."

"Do you want to get something off your chest Sarge?

You've not been your usual alert self today. Is there something bothering you?" he asked, with concern in his voice.

She looked steadily at him for a few moments, weighing up whether to to mention the previous night, then she came to a decision.

"You're a very perceptive man Gary Dean. Actually, there is something but I was reluctant to say anything to anyone in case I sounded daft or paranoid."

"I won't think you're daft Lottie, you can tell me," he encouraged her.

So she told him about being followed the night before and the other times and they discussed anyone who might have a grudge and who had been released from prison recently.

"I've gone over and over it in my mind and I can't think of anyone." She sighed heavily, "maybe it is just my imagination."

"Nah Lottie, you're not the kind of person given to flights of fancy. I've always considered you to be a person with her feet firmly on the ground. And you said Dolly was on high alert, if you don't trust yourself, trust your dog," Dean reassured her. "Why don't you get a hold of the village's CCTV footage? See if that throws any light on it."

"I'm afraid there aren't any CCTV cameras in the village Gary which, in one sense is reassuring since Norham is obviously considered to be a safe place, but not much help to me in this situation.'

"That's a shame," Dean said, "but if anything like that happens again, call the local Bobbies, promise?"

"Okay, I promise."

. . .

WHEN PC'S WHEATFIELD and Wright arrived back in the office around four-thirty, Lottie told them to write up their report ready for the briefing in the morning and then call it a day.

"It's been a long day for everyone so when you've done that get some rest and be fresh for the morning briefing which will be taken by DI Clelland at eight-thirty sharp."

Forty minutes later both Gillian and Jason logged off their computers and put on their jackets.

"Night Sarge," they said and left the office.

"What about you?" Dean asked, putting on his Barbour jacket, a purchase from his better-off days before the separation.

"I won't be far behind you Gary, I'm just preparing for tomorrow's briefing then I'm going home to a long bath and a gin and tonic - after I've walked Dolly, of course."

"I'm sure that dog gets tret better than a lot of bairns I know," was his parting comment. Like the Scots, people from Newcastle often refer to children as "bairns".

"You're probably right Gary," she replied, smiling. "Goodnight!"

11

TUESDAY 19TH SEPTEMBER
EDINBURGH

I n a flat in Edinburgh a man sat watching a recording of Monday night's news coverage of the press conference by Northumbria Police in Newcastle. He sat with a self-satisfied smile on his face. He had just watched a replay of Detective Chief Inspector Flynn giving the media an update on the investigation into the murder of Fr Michael Donovan.

Flynn looked earnestly into the BBC News camera and, holding up the group photo of the priest with the boys, he said, "We're appealing to the public to please come forward if they can help us find the cold blooded killer of the old priest. If you know anyone in this photo, or if you were one of the boys in this group, I urge you to come forward so that we can talk to you and eliminate you from our enquiries. Thank you."

Questions were fired at the Inspector: "Is it true the priest was a paedophile?" "Was it a revenge killing?" and many more in that vein, but the inspector merely said, "That's all I can tell you at this time. A further update will be issued in due course. Thank you and goodnight" He walked off the podium to to a barrage of increasingly more bizarre theories.

He played it again, for the fourth time and grinned. "They havenae got a fuckin' clue!" he said to the empty room, "they're nae further forward now than when they found him swingin' on Saturday mornin' an' it's now Tuesday."

He thought back to Friday night and felt a warm glow of achievement and the satisfaction of a job well done, even if he'd had to wait years to do it. He nodded to himself, smiling at how well his plan had worked. "Aye, Ah waited a long time, a' thae long years until the priest had retired an' was livin' far away fae the safety and protection o' the bloody Catholic Church."

He chuckled at his cleverness and how easy it had been to get the old man legless, in fact, he thought, "It was child's play, though no' the kind o' child's play that evil bastard had been daein' for years. Ah knew the greedy bugger wouldnae be able tae refuse the single malt - his breath used tae reek o' it at times." He'd taken a bottle of expensive malt whisky and held it up tantalisingly in front of the priest when Donovan had opened the door to him.

"Hello Fr Donovan," he'd said, "surely you must remember me?"

The old man peered at him, trying hard to remember, and not wanting to admit to his failing memory.

"St Andrew's 1986? Michael Kelly? Ye had a particular fondness for me, you said, because I was your namesake."

"Of course, of course. Come in," and he led the way into his cosy living room.

Michael stood in the middle of the room, taking in the comfort and expensive furnishings.

"Sit down Michael and let me have a proper look at

you," said Donovan as he sat down on his armchair by the softly glowing fire, a hint of the old lasciviousness in his still expressive face, although his libido had long since departed. He looked at the bottle still clutched in Kelly's hand and unconsciously licked his lips.

Kelly reached out, offering the bottle to the priest and said, "I brought you this for old times sake Father."

The old man moved with surprising alacrity and took the bottle from Michael Kelly. "I'll get some glasses," he said.

He had returned with two beautiful Waterford Crystal whisky tumblers and Michael didn't miss the quality of the man's possessions. He remembered how the priest always seemed to have nice things, especially cars of the sporty variety. He'd been a vain man then and was still a vain man now, he concluded.

The priest poured out a generous measure into the first glass and was about to do the same with the other when Michael said, "Just a very small amount for me Father - I'm driving," he added by way of explanation.

"Thank you," he said, as Donovan handed him the glass. Once the old man had sat down again he raised his glass and said, "Here's to old times Father!"

"Indeed, to old times," replied the priest, raising the glass to his lips.

"How long have you lived here and when did you retire Father?" Michael Kelly asked.

He only pretended to drink the whisky as the priest rambled on about his retiral service at St Mary's Cathedral in Edinburgh and all the dignitaries from the church who had attended it. He tuned out the old man's droning voice and instead focused on the large framed photograph on the mantlepiece, which was in his direct line of vision.

He was right in the centre of the group. The nine year old boy, his dark hair and blue eyes a picture of innocence. An innocence he had been systematically robbed of, at that time, by the man sitting opposite him, the man who'd raped so many innocent boys and made them feel that they had led him on and that they were the shameful, lustful ones.

But he was here for only one boy, the one he was looking at and remembering as he had been before the grooming had started. He controlled his latent anger. He needed to be cold and calm if he was to succeed in his mission. His time spent on the island doing the recce on the priest and his home had paid off and he was not about to fall at the last hurdle.

He had feigned interest in the priest's self-centred, one-sided conversation and had encouraged him to have glass after glass of the smooth, golden liquid. He even poured it himself, when the old man was incapable, and held the glass to his lips coaxing him to keep drinking.

It was only when he was sure Donovan was unconscious with the drink that he set about what he had come for; what he had patiently waited long years to do.

He took the rope out of his small backpack and stood behind the old man's chair, looped it around his neck and pulled. The old man put up no resistance, he was too far gone for that, although there was the sudden and unexpected, ragged gasp as the last of the air in his lungs was expelled and which startled Kelly for a moment or two before he realised the priest was dead.

He came back to the present and stared at the paused TV screen where the DCI was frozen in his address to the press conference. What was it they said about revenge?

"Ah yes," he sighed with deep satisfaction, "Revenge is a dish best served cold". Then he pressed 'play' on the remote control, wanting to watch the efforts of the hapless police inspector once again.

12

WEDNESDAY 20TH SEPTEMBER
TEAM BRIEFING

D I Denise Clelland was studying the updated murder boards when the team filed into the room carrying mugs of tea and coffee to sustain them through the briefing. She turned as the last person closed the door.

"Good morning," she said, "I can see you've been busy since I was last here." She looked around the room and smiled. "So, what do we have to work on now? Are we any closer to catching our killer?" She looked at Lottie, "DS Lockhart?"

Lottie walked up to the board and pointed to the still image of the 4x4 caught on the ANPR footage. "I found the vehicle arriving by the earlier tide, before the causeway was cut off at 13.55. So he was presumably on the island for about twelve hours, possibly getting his bearings and watching the priest's cottage before gaining entry and killing him."

"Any theories as to what happened? There was no forced entry so he was obviously known to Fr Donovan," Clelland said.

"One scenario might be, given the forensic results on the alcohol consumed, that Fr Donovan's visitor was someone he knew from the past, but also someone he had no reason to fear," Lottie began. "The neighbours, Mr and Mrs Smith next door, said they saw no one at his cottage during the day, so it's likely the perpetrator arrived much later, after Mr Smith had gone to the pub and Mrs Smith had closed the curtains and was watching TV."

She paused and looked at the board, then said, "Mr Smith told us that he only saw the car outside the priest's cottage when he came home at around ten o'clock. So, I'm thinking the killer arrived mid-evening and slowly got the priest drunk, hence there being no defensive wounds plus the substantial amount of alcohol in his blood."

"It's a hypothesis that fits in with the forensic report but we don't have witnesses or CCTV to identify anyone - not yet anyway. Go on."

"DC Dean identified the Toyota Land Cruiser heading north on the A1 at 02.00 hours on Saturday morning, he got a partial registration as the vehicle was pretty mucky. He followed it up and now has more information on it." Lottie and the DI both looked at Dean. Lottie sat down and Dean took over.

"Boss," he said, nodding to Clelland. "As you can see, the vehicle was registered in Edinburgh between March and September of 2008. Information gathered from DVLA gave me the names of twelve people with this particular model of car with SK registration plates."

He pointed to the photo on the board. "I started calling everyone on the list and got lucky with the fifth person I spoke to. His car was stolen some time early on Friday morning from his home in Craigentinny, but he only discovered it was missing when he left to go to work on a back shift around one-thirty in the afternoon."

PC Wright guffawed, incredulous, "Ye mean he never noticed it was missing until then?"

"Apparently his windows don't overlook where he parks the car and it was obviously on the island by the time it was reported to the police," Dean replied, trying to hide his impatience with his young colleague.

DI Clelland looked severely at Wright who reddened, mumbled "Sorry" and then carefully studied his hands.

Dean continued, "The car was discovered partially burnt-out on wasteland between Craigmillar and Edinburgh Royal Infirmary at Little France. The car was confirmed as the one stolen by the number on its chassis."

"Thank you Gary," said Clelland, "that's good work. So we can speculate that the driver of the stolen Toyota went to see the priest with murder in mind. He knew that the car could not be traced to him. ..." she groaned in frustration, "and we still have no bloody idea what he looks like, thanks to the lack of CCTV on Holy Island."

She looked around the room and, in a calmer voice, said, "Okay, we can only work with what we've got which, at this point in time is very little other than SOCO's claim the assailant had one leg longer than the other and wore a size 11 Caterpillar boot. I wonder how many of the population that includes!"

She stood silent for some time then said, "So what's next DS Lockhart?"

"PCs Wheatfield and Wright were in Edinburgh yesterday looking at the records for the period Donovan was curate in each parish." She turned to PC Wheatfield and said, "Gillian?"

PC Wheatfield stood up, clasping a sheaf of papers. "Boss," she said, nodding to Lottie, "We spoke to the secretaries in all four parishes and we were able to go through the relevant records for the period in question. Thankfully, they've got all of their records on computer files now and once we'd identified what we were looking for, I was able to email the information here." She handed some stapled sheets to both the DI and DS.

"It's a fairly long list - around thirty names, although it could have been longer but Fr Donovan stopped taking the choir in 2000, so this list," she held it up, "covers a period of about fifteen years."

"Do you know why he ceased teaching the choir then?" Clelland asked.

"No Ma'am, we were just told that he had finished having responsibility for the choir by the millennium," she replied.

"Did you manage to get any other information on the priest Gillian?" Lottie asked.

"Not much Sarge," Gillian said, "nothing further on Fr Donovan, just the names, dates of birth and contact details for the boys at the time."

"Thank you PC's Wheatfield and Wright, that's very helpful," said the DI, "but if the photo from the mantlepiece is as significant as we believe it to be, then the list for that year is where we start."

She turned to Lottie again, "Do we have anything else from yesterday?"

"Yes Ma'am, a call was put through to me from a member of the public, a Dr McGuire, who wanted to give us information on a possible suspect but he refused to say any more over the phone."

"Do you think this person is genuine or a crank caller, as

so many are in these investigations." Clelland asked without much enthusiasm.

"Oh he's genuine alright," Lottie replied, "we checked him out. He's a senior lecturer in Social Policy at Edinburgh University and DC Dean and I are meeting with him later this morning at the university."

The DI's eyes widened and she smiled, "Let's hope this is the lead we're so desperate for, since, at the moment, it feels like we're wading through treacle."

"Well, he said he thinks he knows who killed the priest," Lottie informed her.

DI Clelland stood in thought for several moments while her team watched her expectantly. Finally she said, "Okay, today's tasks are as follows: I will arrange for a warrant to access Michael Donovan's personnel record at the Diocesan Office in Edinburgh. That might throw some light on why he suddenly, or apparently abruptly, stopped taking choir practice."

She began to pace the room. "Meanwhile, I want you, PC Wheatfield, to access the priest's bank account, see if there was anything suspicious going on there. What do we have on his phone records?"

"The tech guys should be getting a log of his calls and texts to us by this afternoon Ma'am," Dean replied.

"Okay, great. PC Wright. I know it's tedious but murders are mainly solved with good old fashioned detective work."

Wright looked up, willingness spread across his face, "Ma'am?" he said, still ready and willing to play his part in his first murder enquiry.

"I'd like you to go through the list of boys, starting with those around in 1986, use the contact details you have, see if you can find out where they are now. Check schools and HMRC if you have to, I want them TIE'd."

"Ah'm on it Ma'am," he replied, writing in his notebook.

She checked her watch and said, "I want everyone back here by five o'clock sharp with everything you have by then.

As the others rose to leave the room, she called Lockhart and Dean over. "Call me as soon as you've finished your meeting with Dr McGuire. If we're in luck we can have this person brought in for questioning ASAP. Good luck!"

13

WEDNESDAY 20TH SEPTEMBER
EDINBURGH

G ary drove as Lottie navigated their way to the university once they'd come off the City Bypass in the stop-start traffic at the Newcraighall exit. She directed him to turn left into Buccleuch Place where there was meter parking.

They pulled up in a parking bay and Lottie read the prices on the meter. "Good grief!" she cried incredulous, "£9.80 for two hours? We just want to park not buy a piece of the street!"

"That's Edinburgh prices for you," Gary laughed, glad that the money wasn't coming from his own impecunious pocket, "you're spoiled in Norham and Berwick with your free parking!"

Lottie fed five two pound coins into the meter and carefully displayed the ticket, having eyed an enthusiastic traffic warden further along the street.

"Who could afford to park here every day?" she asked when she got back to the car, still stunned at the cost.

Gary checked his watch and said, "Perfect timing, it's

eleven twenty-five. Let's go and see what Dr McGuire has to say."

They climbed the steps from Buccleuch Place to George Square where the Adam Ferguson Building was situated on the south side of George Square Garden. The Garden was a verdant, tranquil haven, for staff and students alike, amidst the bustle of university life.

They entered the building and approached a servitor who directed them to Dr McGuire's office on the first floor. Dr McGuire was hovering in the corridor awaiting their arrival. He looked anxious.

"Dr McGuire?" enquired Lottie, "I'm DS Lockhart and this is DC Dean."

They shook hands and Dr McGuire said, "Thank you for agreeing to see me here, it would have been impossible for me to get away so early in the new academic year."

"That's no problem Sir," Lottie said, trying to put him at his ease, "I believe you have some information for us regarding the person who may have been responsible for the murder of Fr Michael Donovan?"

"Yes, yes. Please do come in and sit down," he hurried into the room he'd been standing outside when they'd entered the corridor. "Would you like some tea or coffee?"

Before Lottie could refuse for them both, Dean said, "That would be champion, tea please, with milk, no sugar."

Lottie thought she might as well have one if the man was going to to the trouble of putting the kettle on, besides, she was thirsty. She said, "Tea for me too please Dr McGuire - same as DC Dean's."

While he busied himself with the kettle and mugs, Lottie looked around the bright airy room. A window, the entire width of one wall faced south and looked out onto the street where they'd parked.

The other walls were lined from floor to ceiling with shelves filled with books and box files. They were seated in low comfortable chairs in a corner area which was obviously set up to accommodate meetings and tutorials.

When Dr McGuire sat down beside them, Lottie said, "You told me yesterday that you think you know who killed Fr Donovan. Do you have a name for this person Sir?"

"Yes, I do. It goes back to July, we - that's two acquaintances and I - had a meeting to discuss how to go about getting some redress for what Fr Donovan had done ... at the time I thought Phil was just mouthing off." He ran his hand through his hair, clearly distressed "... then I forgot all about it until I saw the news about the murder."

"Just take your time Sir," Lottie said soothingly. Dean was taking notes, as usual. He had studied shorthand when he first joined the police and found it invaluable for verbatim note-taking.

"There were three of us who had made formal complaints to the Catholic Church about Fr Donovan abusing us when we were choir boys. There are probably many more who were abused but the three of us were in St Andrew's Church choir at the same time. Each of us thought that we were alone in what was happening."

He paused, trying to marshal his thoughts. "The response we got from the Diocesan Office said that without evidence, i.e. someone who had witnessed the *alleged abuse*," he made punctuation marks in the air, "there was nothing they could do about it and they made it clear that no further action would be taken in the matter."

"When was this Dr McGuire?" Lottie asked.

"Three and a half, nearly four years ago. Just before Covid, then with lockdown it went onto the back burner, as it were."

"And when did the matter surface again Sir?"

"It would be the end of June, maybe the beginning of July, when I got a text message from Phil asking me to set up a meeting for the three of us who'd made the formal complaints," John McGuire said, looking out of the window and trying to remember the exact details.

"We met at my flat around the middle of July." He went on to describe how they discussed their options to take the complaint against the priest further and to try to get some justice or reparation and how the meeting was brought to an abrupt end by Phil.

"He told us, in a rather unnervingly cold, quiet voice that there was one option that we had not considered and when we asked him what that was, he said, "Murder the bastard." Then he got up and left."

He sat for some moments in silent reflection, then said, "We've all suffered in one way or another over the years, experiencing something like that in childhood does affect one's mental health, but I think it affected Phil more than either Martin or me because he wasn't in a position to afford counselling." He shook his head sadly, "He lost his wife and children because of the bouts of depression." Dean stiffened momentarily as the man could have been talking about him.

McGuire went on, "It affected him badly during his school years and he had a lot of time off sick. He got almost no qualifications and did a number of manual jobs. He now drives a black cab and he told us, that day, that he struggles to make ends meet. Do you think that's what pushed him over the edge?" He looked at the detectives expectantly.

"We don't know that it was him who killed the priest. We need more than a threat a couple of months ago to be able to charge him with that," Lottie explained.

"Yes, of course, I'm just a bit overwrought at the possibility that a meeting in my home might have triggered such a terrible thing. I wanted Donovan brought to justice, not dead."

"I understand Dr McGuire and we will make enquiries. Have you spoken to either of the men since that meeting?"

"I haven't seen either of them since, although I sent a text to Martin to let him know that I had contacted you."

He gave Lottie the mobile numbers for Philip Hughes and Martin Davidson. "Do you have addresses for them Sir?" Lottie asked.

"No, but Philip lives in a flat in Gorgie Road, I've dropped him off there once or twice. It's in a tenement near the Hearts football ground. Sorry, I don't know the stair number."

"Thank you, and Mr Davidson?"

"He lives in Baberton, again I don't know the address," he broke off and looked at them. "We weren't friends, we just had a mission in common. Martin works in management at the Royal Bank of Scotland, he's based in St Andrew's Square I think."

"That's very helpful Dr McGuire and can you tell us where you were during the day on Friday the 15th of September until the early hours of Saturday morning?" Lottie asked, trying to sound friendly.

He looked shocked as he realised what the question implied.

"We have to ask everyone Sir, it's part of our routine enquiries." She smiled reassuringly.

"I was here all day - that can be verified by any number of students who attended my lectures throughout the day. Then, in the evening we had friends round for dinner. I can let you have their details for verification." He wrote down the names and contact details of his friends and handed it to Lottie.

"Thank you Dr McGuire, you've been very helpful." She looked at Dean and they both stood up.

She handed McGuire her business card and said, "If you think of anything else, please don't hesitate to contact me."

They shook hands and he said, "I'll show you out."

"No need to Sir," Lottie replied, "we'll find our way, we've taken up enough of your time as it is."

He watched them walk along the corridor to the stairs then closed the door. He walked over to the window with a deeply felt weariness and stood looking out, unseeing, for a long time.

Back in the car Lottie called the DI and gave her the information they'd been given. "While we're here do you want us to go to the bank and talk to Martin Davidson?"

Clelland was silent for a few moments then said, "No Lottie, he's not a priority, a phone call will do in the first instance. Get yourselves back here and make a start on tracking down the man who made the threat."

"Will do Ma'am," she replied and hung up. "Back to base Gary, we need to track down Mr Hughes."

14

WEDNESDAY AFTERNOON
INCIDENT ROOM, BERWICK

W hen DI Clelland finished her phone call with Lottie, she went over to the desks where PC's Wheatfield and Wright were busy working through their tasks.

"Jason check your list for a Philip Hughes," she said, looking at the paper on which she'd written down the information that Lottie had given her.

"Found it Ma'am," he said, "he was a choir and altar boy in St Andrew's from 1986-88."

"Do you have an address for him?"

"Eh ..." he ran his finger along the page, "yep, 17 Telford Drive, Edinburgh."

She checked her notes then said, "Well he doesn't live there now, but check directory enquiries, his parents might still live there - if they're still alive - you just might get lucky."

"Will do Ma'am," he got up to get an Edinburgh phone book from the general office downstairs..

"How are you doing Gillian?" she asked.

"There was a Royal Bank of Scotland debit card in with

the box of personal effects the SOCOs removed from the cottage and I contacted the branch in Edinburgh where Fr Donovan had his account," she began. The DI wanted her to get straight to the point, but after working with her over the past five days, she knew the woman was meticulous and would get there in her own time.

"After several calls to verify who I was, they agreed to send over his bank statements for the past five years." She pointed to a sheaf of papers on her desk which had several transactions highlighted in fluorescent orange.

The DI leaned over to look at them and saw that regular monthly payments of two hundred and fifty pounds were paid out, with the reference "Donation" beside it.

"Get on to the bank Gillian and find out who the recipient of this generous donation is."

"Ma'am," replied Gillian.

Jason returned with the phone book as Clelland went back to her office. "God, dae ye ken how many Hugheses there are Gillian?" he asked.

"Think yourself lucky it's not Smith you're looking for," Gillian replied with a chuckle.

"Aye, ye're right enough," smiled the irrepressible Jason as he laboriously went through the list.

After a few minutes he exclaimed, "Bingo!" and proceeded to dial a number. After around twenty rings, and just as he was about to hang up, the phone was answered by a woman with a thin, reedy voice.

"Hallo, Hallo!" she said.

"Good afternoon!" Jason said, "is that Mrs Hughes?"

"What's that son?" she asked in a tremolo voice, "ye'll have tae speak up as Ah'm a wee bit deaf."

"A *wee* bit deaf!" Jason said under his breath, then

Gillian, who was on the phone to the bank, gave him one of her looks.

He spoke louder this time, "Are you Mrs Hughes?"

"Aye son, who are you?" she asked.

He told her who he was and before he could say anything else, she cried, "The polis! What dae the polis want wi' me?"

After much repetition and explanation and reassuring her that it was just a routine enquiry, he waited while she got her address book for her son's address.

"Are ye still there?" she asked when she picked up the phone again. "He's moved that many times these past few years that Ah've lost track," she explained, "Have ye got a pencil and paper handy?"

Jason said he had and wrote down the address. "Thank you very much for your help Mrs Hughes," he said, annunciating each word clearly and at volume.

"Result!" he said to Gillian, who had finished her call.

Just then Lockhart and Dean returned and they went straight to Clelland's office to give her a full account of their meeting in Edinburgh.

15

EVENING BRIEFING

The members of the Murder Investigating Team were sitting in a semi-circle in front of the murder boards when DI Clelland entered the room. The boards had been updated with the names of potential suspects.

"Alright team, I know that you've been busy and had a productive day," she began, "so, what more do we know now?" She turned to Jason, "PC Wright, what progress have you made with the list of choir boys?"

"It's as Ah thought Ma'am. Some of the boys on this list now live in various parts o' the world: one is in the States; two are in Canada; one is in New Zealand and one has died, so we can safely rule them out," he said looking pleased with himself. "And Ah've got contact details for the remaining twenty-five and can report that seven of them are scattered throughout the UK." He looked at the DI, hoping for praise.

"That's good work Jason, thank you. How many have you managed to speak to so far?"

"Ah'm still working my way through the list and some

went right onto answer phone so Ah've left messages asking them to get back to me ASAP."

"Good. Am I correct in thinking there are eighteen of the boys on the list still living in Edinburgh?"

"Edinburgh and the Lothians Ma'am with one," he checked his list, "across the water in Fife."

"So we prioritise those men and if nothing comes from that, we need to look further afield since it's possible that the driver of the stolen Toyota ditched the car and travelled onwards via public transport, or his own car left in the city for his return."

She turned to Gillian next. "PC Wheatfield, you were looking at the victim's bank accounts, tell us what you've got."

"Ma'am," she said, "Fr Donovan's bank statements were pretty much the usual transactions for shopping, petrol and utilities, with the exception of a regular monthly payment for two hundred and fifty pounds with the bank reference as "Donation"."

Clelland, who already knew all this, wished she'd just tell them what she'd found out but she curbed her impatience.

"When I called the bank for clarification of who the payee was, they told me it went into the account of a James McMahon. It's an Edinburgh account and it's been paid into the account for the past two and a half years."

"Is James McMahon on your list Jason?" Clelland asked.

"Yes Ma'am," he said, double checking to be sure. The DI added the name to the board.

"Are ye sayin' he was blackmailing the priest?" asked an incredulous Jason.

"What else could it be Jason?" asked the DI.

PC Wright sat looking puzzled for a few moments then

said, "But Ah can't see him being our killer, Ah mean, ye wouldnae kill the goose that lays the golden egg, would ye?"

"Good point Jason, but unless this was a regular payment by the priest for philanthropic reasons, then I think we're looking at blackmail and, since blackmail is a crime - and if this is blackmail - it was committed outside our area, then we have to pass it on to Police Scotland to investigate."

She looked at Lottie, "DS Lockhart would you please arrange that?" As an afterthought she added, "and get them to check where he was on Friday the 15th of September."

"Yes Ma'm," Lottie said, then she gave the team an account of the meeting of the three men in July that Dr McGuire had told them about. While she was doing that the DI was writing Philip Hughes name above McMahon's under the heading POI, (Persons Of Interest), with Police Scotland in brackets beside McMahon's name.

"You were looking at the priest's mobile phone record DC Dean, did the techies get back to you?" Clelland spoke to Gary next.

"Yes Ma'am, there was a call log sheet waiting for me when I got back from Edinburgh," he said, looking at the sheet, "and the only thing that stands out is that it has very few calls out or in. Like many older people, I don't think Fr Donovan liked new technology and he probably kept it for emergencies only."

"Thank you Gary," said Clelland, "do we have an address for Philip Hughes?"

"Ma'am," Jason replied, raising his hand, "Ah spoke to his mother this afternoon and, at the moment, he lives in a flat at 182 Gorgie Road, Edinburgh. She said he moves around a lot."

Lottie put her hand up and said, "Dr McGuire

mentioned that he drives a black taxi so I was thinking that it might prove difficult to catch him at home. It might be easier, and quicker, if we contacted the black taxi companies to find out which one he drives for and intercept him that way?"

"Good point Lottie, I'll leave that with you, shall I? Does anyone else want to add anything?"

Nobody did, so she continued, "To summarise then ..." she turned to look at the boards for several seconds, gathering her thoughts. "We have at least two people of particular interest who need to be tracked down and interviewed as a priority - Philip Hughes and James McMahon, who, as I said earlier, Police Scotland will deal with."

She began pacing as she always found this helpful when analysing information. "Martin Davidson also needs to be interviewed since he was a member of the trio with a grudge and who was at that meeting in July. We need to know where they all were all day on the Friday." She stopped and she tapped the photo of the scene at the Priory, "until the early hours of Saturday morning."

She looked at Lottie and Gary, "I want you both to take care of that."

"Ma'am," Lottie said adding this to her list of tasks.

The DI continued, "We need fingerprints from all of them to compare with those taken at the murder scene since there is no match for them on our system."

Lottie raised her hand and Clelland nodded for her to speak, "Ma'am, I was thinking that since the killer was willing to leave his fingerprints behind it might suggest that he is either is bit dim or he thinks he's committed the perfect murder and won't be caught, in which case he's also arrogant and he believes he can remain, under our radar."

"And so far he's right, isn't he? What are we missing?"

She asked of no one in particular. She looked at the boards again and ran her hand through her hair, frustration showing in every movement.

"Gillian, I want you and Jason to speak to everyone on that list and get their agreement to have their fingerprints taken - wherever they are in the UK. We need to eliminate as many men on that list as possible and narrow down the pool of potential suspects."

"Ma'am," Gillian replied.

Clelland looked around the room with a grim expression and said, "We need a breakthrough soon. The DCI is under pressure from those above him and he's threatening to hand the case over to another team. Tomorrow is make or break time, I can't emphasise that enough."

There was a murmur of shock in the room, then she added, "Look, I know everyone is working extremely hard and you're all doing your best, but this case poses an extra challenge with so many potential suspects, scattered who knows where, and who might all have a strong motive for killing the priest."

Dean, who had been sitting looking increasingly puzzled while the DI was talking, raised his hand.

Clelland nodded and he said, "Ma'am, why wait until now? Most of these men are in their forties, so why wait until now to kill the priest, all these years later, I mean?"

"That's a good question DC Dean and we will only know the answer to that when we have our man."

"Revenge," piped up PC Wright.

"Yeah Jason," replied Dean, "but why now?"

"Because," said Jason with a sudden insight, "*revenge is a dish best served cold*, as the saying goes."

Clelland just shrugged her shoulders. She looked tired

and a shade defeated. "Okay team," she said with a big sigh, "go home now. Rest and come back fresh in the morning."

There were replies of "Will do" and "Yes Ma'am" as they gathered their belongings and left for the day.

As Lottie and Gary walked together to the car park, he said, "I feel bad that we are now five days into this investigation and we're not much further forward. What *are* we missing Lottie?"

"Well Gary, as you said earlier, the killer might think he's committed the perfect crime, is arrogant enough to leave his fingerprints behind in the belief that we won't be able to trace him, so, the question is: is he very clever or very stupid?"

"Maybe he's clever." Gary replied, "remember at the very beginning of this investigation, we said we must keep an open mind and that the paedophile thing might be to throw us off?"

"You think we're going down a blind alley?"

"Maybe." he said.

Lottie thought for some moments then said, "I'm going back to talk to the DI, I'll see you in the morning Gary." and she turned and hurried back to the station to catch Clelland before she headed back to Newcastle. She wanted to remind the DI about keeping an open mind and not getting blinkered by the 'paedophile' message and a single line of enquiry.

16

HONEY BEE COTTAGE

THAT EVENING

Norham

It was seven o'clock by the time Lottie got home and the sun had already set behind the hills across the border in Scotland. It had been a long tiring day and all Lottie wanted to do was walk Dolly, get some supper and have an early night.

She unlocked the front door to her cottage and was about to step into the small vestibule when the door stuck against something lying behind it. She thought it must be an Amazon delivery so she pushed harder and stepped inside.

Dolly normally met her at the door, tail wagging but the house was silent and she thought Dolly must be with Jane, next door. As she closed the door she saw what was lying behind it and gasped, jumping back in alarm. Lying on the floor was a seventy centimetre long adder and it was dead. She recognised the tell-tale zig-zag pattern down its back from the rare occasions she had spotted one on woodland walks.

Knowing they were venomous, she rushed through the cottage to make sure that Dolly was alright. Then she checked herself, tutting, "It's dead you silly woman and Dolly must be with Jane."

She went back along the hallway towards the front door and, despite knowing the snake was dead, she gave it a wide berth and hurried next door to Jane's cottage, her heart still thudding in her ribcage.

Jane opened the door quickly and said, "Oh Lottie, I was looking out for you, I wanted to catch you before you went into the house, but I see I'm too late." She took in Lottie's pale face. "Come in, you've had an awful shock."

On hearing Lottie's name, Dolly bounced along the hall and greeted Lottie with her usual exuberance, tail windmilling as she snuffled Lottie's hand.

They went into Jane's comfortable sitting room and Jane poured Lottie a glass of brandy. "Sip this slowly and I'll tell you what happened."

Lottie took the proffered drink gratefully and waited for Jane to speak.

"It was about six-thirty and it wasn't long since I had come back from giving Dolly her dinner when there was an almighty barking from her, so I got your back door key and went in through your kitchen." Jane began her tale.

"I called for Dolly but she didn't come, so I knew that something was wrong as she usually rushes into the kitchen on hearing me at the back door."

She poured herself a small brandy then sat down in her chair by the fire and continued. "When I came through I found Dolly standing rigid in the hallway, hackles high. I switched the light on and that's when I saw what had frightened her. I knew the snake was dead because it wasn't moving."

"Well thank God it was dead," Lottie said, "otherwise Dolly might have been bitten."

"Indeed," agreed Jane "but I couldn't touch the thing Lottie. I just got Dolly out and came back here as fast as I could. I wanted to catch you before you went in and discovered it."

She shuddered, "I wasn't sure whether to call the police, but it's not my home to be taking that kind of liberty Pet," Jane said, shaking her mop of white curls. "I tried calling you but you must have been on your way home as your mobile went straight to voice mail."

"It's alright Jane, I usually have it switched off when I'm driving." Lottie sat thinking about what she should do, then said, "I suppose I should report it."

"But who would do such a thing? And why? Do you think it might have been one of the village youths trying to scare you?"

"I don't know Jane, I wouldn't have thought so. They've always been pleasant anytime I've seen them in the village when I've been out with Dolly," Lottie said, not wanting to frighten her friend by telling her about being followed. "I'll call the police," she decided, "and wait here until they arrive, if that's okay with you?"

"Of course it is Pet."

Half an hour later, two uniformed officers knocked on Jane's door and Lottie told them about discovering the snake when she got home from work. The officers, who knew her from Berwick police station, were very reassuring.

While Dolly stayed with Jane she took them into her cottage by the back door to cause less disturbance at the front door crime scene.

Lottie stayed in the living room while they examined the area around the front door and the snake, wearing nitrile gloves to protect any fingerprint evidence.

Lottie was just making tea for them all when the female officer, PC Melville, came into the kitchen. She said, "You've had a right fright Ma'am, but try not to worry. Tom will remove the snake and we'll get SOCOs out to dust for prints."

Just then Tom, PC Williams joined them. "Tea?" Lottie asked, "while you take my statement."

"That would be champion Ma'am," said Tom.

Lottie indicated the sofa for them to sit down and, amidst the crackling and background chatter from the radios on their shoulders, they took a full statement from her.

"It's a good thing the snake was already dead," PC Melville said, "as I wouldn't like the thought of your dog being attacked."

Lottie shuddered and said, "I know, poor Dolly must have got such a fright."

Tom put his notebook away and said, "Can you avoid using the front door for the time being Ma'am, I'll call the SOCOs now but I don't know when they'll get here, but hopefully it'll be tonight."

Lottie laughed, without mirth, "No, problem," she said, "I don't want to see that thing again. What will you do with it, by the way?"

"We'll bag it and take it to the station as evidence."

"Of course, how stupid of me, I should know that, but obviously I'm not thinking straight as it's not the usual delivery you find behind your front door."

They all got up and, after Tom had collected the snake, Lottie showed them out the back door. "Thank you for coming so promptly officers" she said, "You've been very reassuring."

"You're welcome Ma'am, we'll just ask around your neighbours, see if anyone saw someone at your door around six-thirty."

IT WAS nine-thirty by the time the SOCOs had finished. It was Anna, Tim Lightfoot's assistant, who Lottie had met only briefly before.

"I'm sorry to say say that whoever put the snake through your letterbox must have used gloves, so no fingerprints." Lottie's heart sank.

"However, I have managed to lift glove prints and I'll check them on the database when I get back. Some types of sports gloves have their own particular markings on the finger pads, although it won't help us much in identifying the culprit, but it can be logged for future reference."

It was ten-thirty when Lottie finally sat down after she'd collected Dolly from Jane's and she had well and truly lost her appetite. She could only face some tea and toast.

"Well Dolly," she said, as Dolly stretched out on the sofa next to her, "that decides it. Tomorrow I'm going to order CCTV to be installed at both the front and back doors and bugger the expense."

Dolly just moaned under her breath by way of response. Like Lottie, she'd had more than enough excitement for one day.

As she sat in the quiet of her home, Lottie wondered again who was following her. The fact that they knew exactly where she lived was a disturbing thought. "And who would be so nasty as to put a dead snake through her door?"

Exhausted, she got up and put her supper dishes in the

sink, thinking they would just have to wait until morning to be washed. She went to bed, expecting to be awake with worry or nightmares involving snakes. Instead, she fell into a deep, restful sleep and did not waken until her alarm went off at six-thirty.

17

WEDNESDAY EVENING

GARY

A s Lottie hurried back to the station to speak to the DI, Gary's phone rang. He looked at the caller ID and his heart sank, it was Shirley.

"Shit! That's all I need," he said, trying to decide whether to answer it or to let it go to voicemail.

It was still ringing when he got into the car so he tapped the green 'accept' button.

"You took your time answering," she said, already on the attack.

He was immediately on the alert in case something had happened to his daughters. "What's wrong? Are the girls alright?" he asked.

"Ellie and Poppy are fine. I need to talk to you about something, can you come here?"

"What now? I'm still in Berwick, I've just finished work Shirley and I'm tired," he explained, "can't it wait?" He had calmed down now that he knew his daughters were okay.

"No Gary," she said in exasperation, "it can't wait. I need to talk to you tonight."

"Can't you tell me what it is over the phone, if it's so

urgent?" He would like nothing better than to see his daughters but not when he was so tired.

"Look, please yourself then," she said, "I'm actually doing you a favour as the twins' father. I don't need your permission, but I thought I'd extend you the courtesy of informing you that Joules will be moving in with us at the weekend."

This was a bolt from the blue. He sat so long in stunned silence, outraged thoughts tripping over each other.

"Gary! Are you still there?"

"And when was this decided? It obviously isn't a spur of the moment decision," he raged, "Shirley, this is not going to happen, I'm not having a stranger living in the same house as my bairns!" he told her unequivocally.

"Gary, listen to me, it is going to happen and it's happening this weekend!" she told him with a smugness that enraged him further.

She had always got her own way, from choosing names for the girls to their home furnishings. She never consulted him, she *informed* him.

He sighed heavily, looked at his watch and said, "I'll be there within the hour," and he hung up amidst her protests about him entering *her* home in an angry state.

He drove at just above the speed limit during the entire journey, vaguely aware of the road ahead and the other traffic. When he arrived in Gosforth he realised he must have been on automatic and was relieved that he hadn't been stopped for speeding.

Dusk was deepening as he sat outside his former home and feelings of homesickness overwhelmed him. Shirley hadn't yet closed the curtains and he could see the warm, homely glow of lamps through the large window of the lounge.

Shirley was sitting in an armchair reading a magazine and there were no other lights on in the house. He thought she must have sent the children to bed early when he'd said he was coming to the house after all.

He got wearily out of the car, feeling bone tired. He took a deep breath in preparation for the battle to come then he walked up the path and rang the doorbell. He had surrendered his keys to Shirley, at her insistence, when he left the family home.

She opened the door, unsmiling and with no greeting. She just turned and walked along the hallway to the lounge, leaving him to close the door behind him. She sat on the armchair she'd just vacated, her mouth a thin line of displeasure, and waited for him to speak.

"Are the bairns in bed already like?" he asked, looking at the clock and seeing it was only eight o'clock.

"They're at my mother's, I didn't want you getting them upset," she replied.

He sighed wearily at the accusation, made before he'd even had the chance to say anything. "I wasn't going to be upsetting them Shirley, can I sit down?"

She nodded to the sofa and he sat down, unzipping his Barbour jacket, the warmth of the room was stifling after the cool air of the evening outside, but he didn't dare to take it off for fear of irritating her further.

She hadn't offered him a drink and he was thirsty, the anxiety about the certain confrontation to come had made his mouth so dry he felt his tongue sticking to the roof of his mouth.

"Do you mind if I have a glass of water?" he asked, getting up off the sofa.

"I'll get it," she said sharply, making it clear that he was only a visitor in the house and an unwanted one at that.

He took a long draught from the glass she'd handed him before speaking. He tried to make his voice conciliatory as he said, "Look Shirley, I know you've been seeing your colleague, but the girls are too young and vulnerable from the separation to be moving him into our home. It'll confuse them."

"*My home*," she snapped, the sound of her voice was like a whip lash.

"Our home," he repeated, "the deeds are still in joint names Shirley, we haven't reached a financial settlement yet."

"And whose fault is that?" she countered.

"Look Shirley," he continued, trying to appease her, his hands were stretched out placatingly, "I agreed that I would move out so as to keep things as normal as possible while Ellie and Poppy got used to the change in circumstances and I didn't mind being in that poky flat at first, as long as I could have the bairns there on visits." He paused, trying to find words that would not inflame this already difficult conversation.

"You then said that it wasn't suitable for overnight stays because there wasn't a second bedroom and when I offered to sleep on the sofa, you dismissed that out of hand."

"Well you can't expect to put them up in that slum you moved into," she said defensively.

"I think we're getting away from the point here Shirley," he said, "All I'm saying is that I've given up all of this ..." he swept his arm around, indicating the house, " ... the home we built up together, just until the girls could get used to me not being here and being a constant part of their lives. I've lost everything that was precious and familiar, but me being in a one bedroom flat was never meant to be permanent."

He stopped as she was clearly not interested. He put his

head in his hands for several moments, wondering how to go on, then he tried appealing to her.

"Look Shirley, surely you can understand I don't want to feel that I'm being replaced in the girls' home and affections. I feel like I've been almost totally shut out of their lives as it is. Why don't you wait until after the divorce settlement instead of rushing in and cohabiting with him?"

"Joules will be moving in here at the weekend," she said, as though she hadn't heard a word he'd said, "so you will just have to live with it. Now, I think we're finished here," she said, getting up from the chair.

"NO!" he shouted, his patience suddenly evaporating, "we are *far* from finished Shirley. I want the house put on the market straight away and I want half of the proceeds of the sale plus half the value of the joint furnishings in this house."

"You can't do that!" She argued, "you agreed when you left that I would stay here with the girls."

"That was a verbal undertaking to give the girls time to come to terms with the separation," he said, his voice so cold that she said nothing. "And I did not leave, you put me out. From now on, we will communicate through our solicitors, but be clear, this house will be sold and I will have access to my children." He left the house without another word.

18

EDINBURGH

THURSDAY 21ST SEPTEMBER

P hilip Hughes sat in an interview room in St Leonard's Police Station. Police Scotland had been happy to accommodate Northumbria Police during the murder investigation.

Hughes had been there for fifteen minutes and he was sure it was a deliberate ploy to unnerve him. In fact, Lockhart and Dean were in conversation with DI Clelland, arranging for Martin Davidson to meet them there in an hour's time.

As he waited, Hughes thought back over the strange events of the last hour. He had been working the day shift when he'd received a message from the radio controller in the taxi company office.

"Car 402 over." he'd answered the call.

"Do you have a fare at the moment Phil?" the controller asked.

"I'm just about to drop off at the Bruntsfield Hotel, over." he replied.

"Put your for hire light off when you've done that and get back to the office ASAP, over."

"What the fuck for? Ah cannae make money in the office." Radio protocol was dropped completely now.

"There are two detectives who want to speak to you Phil, so I suggest you come here after you drop your fare off," said the controller.

"Roger that," Hughes growled and switched off his radio.

When he'd arrived at the taxi company's base he was directed to the back office where two police officers were waiting for him.

"What's this a' aboot?" he asked them, "Ah'm tryin' tae make a livin' an every minute Ah'm no' in ma cab Ah'm losin' money."

Lottie introduced herself and Gary and said in a placatory tone, "Mr. Hughes, we would like to talk to you in connection with the murder of Father Michael Donovan and we would be grateful if you would agree to speak to us informally."

"Am Ah under arrest?" Hughes asked.

"No Sir, but we would like to ask you some questions so we can eliminate you from our enquiries."

"Ah had nothin' tae dae wi' the priest gettin' murdered."

"We're talking to everyone who knew Father Donovan in the 1980's, when he was a curate in Edinburgh," Gary reassured him, "we're not singling you out Mr Hughes, it's all part of our routine enquiries."

Hughes swithered for another few moments then agreed. "Aye fine, Ah've nothin' tae hide, what do you want to know?"

"We have a room in St Leonard's Police Station Sir." Lottie said, then added as voices could be clearly heard in the corridor, "It will be more private than here."

And so, twenty minutes later they were ensconced in

Interview Room 1 in St Leonard's Police Station on Edinburgh's South Side.

Lottie began by asking him to state his full name, address and date of birth.

"Thank you Mr Hughes, we won't keep you longer than necessary and, as I said before, these are routine questions in connection with our investigation into Fr Donovan's murder."

"Aye, Ah understand," replied Hughes, looking at his watch and mourning the fares he was losing, "but can we just get on wi' it?" His earlier antagonism was still apparent.

"Of course Mr Hughes," Lottie agreed, wanting to keep the man on board. "Can you tell me about the meeting you attended in July this year with John McGuire and Martin Davidson?"

His eyes widened as realisation dawned on him and he said, "Ah! So ye ken aboot me sayin' one o' our options tae get justice would be tae kill the bastard?" He grimaced at how a moment's anger had come back to bite him.

"Yes Mr Hughes, we came by this particular piece of information during the course of our enquiries," Lottie said, "but I'd like you to tell me about it from your point of view."

Hughes closed his eyes for a few seconds as he thought back to that stormy Saturday afternoon in Melville Terrace and told the detectives about the difficult years that led up to that point in time.

"My grandparents were from Ireland and my grandfather worked as a navvy diggin' roads. There was a family tradition where the males served as altar boys and, as Ah wis the only boy amongst three sisters, Ah felt it wis ma duty to do that." He began telling them his story.

"Then one day the priest fae St Andrew's Church - that's the church we went to - came to the school lookin' tae recruit boys for the church choir and ma teacher put me forward for that."

"And was that something you yourself wanted Mr Hughes?" Lottie asked.

He considered the question, surprised that he'd never thought about it before himself. "Aye an' no." he said eventually, "Aye because Ah suppose it made me a bit special like, because ma mother was proud o' me gettin' picked fae the whole class. An' no because, at first anyway, Ah didnae ken the other laddies that a' seemed tae ken each other."

"And did you get to know the other boys in the choir?" she asked.

"Kind of, but only durin' choir practice since they were well off an' lived in the same posh area as the church," he explained, "an' we lived in a council hoose in Telford."

Lottie nodded her understanding.

"Sometimes Fr Donovan would gie me a lift home and, on one o' thae occasions he suggested that Ah might want tae have extra, private tuition at the priest's hoose." Then he added, self-mockingly, "because he said Ah was special."

At this point, Dean, who was busy taking the interview down in shorthand, froze, causing Lottie to look at him.

"Go on Mr Hughes," Lottie said gently, knowing he was approaching some emotionally difficult memories.

"Well, nae prizes for guessin' what that turned oot tae be," he laughed, but there was no humour in the laughter. "That's when he started groomin' me - ye know, in thae days there wisnae a word for it, no' like now - but that's what he was daein'." He nodded to himself.

"Can you tell me a bit more about that Mr Hughes?"

"It started wi' presents an' sweeties an' then Ah had tae dae things in return, tae show Ah wis grateful ... until it led tae full-blown sex." He stopped, no longer able to hold

Lottie's eye contact, so she made a show of looking at her hands and he continued. "And in some ways Ah wis grateful for the nice things he gave me, like the Hibs football strip and sometimes he gave me money."

After a few moments silence he went on, anger in his voice now, "But Ah also felt guilt an' shame. He did that! He made me feel like it was ma fault an' that Ah was committin' a mortal sin and ye ken what?" he looked Lottie in the eye again, "That was enough tae make me keep it a secret." He shook his head sadly, "He didnae have tae threaten me, Ah just knew no' tae tell anybody."

Although Lottie did not want to interrupt what was obviously a cathartic experience for this man, she needed to move the interview on. "But the meeting in July suggests that you told John McGuire and Martin Davidson?" she asked.

"Aye, we had all been invited to some do in honour o' Fr Donovan," he said, "Ah cannae remember exactly what it was, but John, Martin an' me left early an' went tae the pub. Well, after a few pints, we somehow discovered that we each thought we had been alone in receiving this *special attention* from the priest."

"Is that when you made the complaint to the Catholic Church?"

"Aye, John drew me up a copy of the complaint an' a' Ah had to do was sign it." But the Church dismissed it and did bugger all about it an' that's what led tae the meetin' in John's hoose in July," he concluded.

"That's when you suggested murdering Fr Donovan, as a way of dealing with the unresolved complaint?" Lottie asked.

"Ach, Ah wis just mouthin' off. Ah'd had a bad few weeks, earnings wise, an' Ah wis really pissed off an' the words just flew out o' ma mouth an' Ah walked oot o' the flat," he told them. "Ah havenae heard fae them since. They probably think it was me that murdered him."

He looked at Lottie and added, "Ah know it sounds like Ah've got a motive for murderin' him, but Ah didnae kill the priest. Ah wis just really angry that day at the way Ah felt ma life was ruined because o' the abuse, but Ah didnae murder him."

Lottie was inclined to believe him but she continued with her questions. "Can you tell me where you were between the hours of one o'clock on the afternoon of Friday the fifteenth of September and two o'clock on the Saturday morning?"

"Ah worked the 6am to 6pm shift on the Friday, like Ah do every day, and then Ah went for a pint at ma local."

"And what's the name of your local Mr Hughes?" Lottie asked.

"The Tynecastle Arms."

"Can anyone vouch for you?"

Hughes laughed, "Aboot half the pub. A bunch o' us taxi drivers meet up on a Friday for a few jars," he said, "ask Brenda, the barmaid, as well, she'll tell ye. Likes tae flirt wi' the men does Brenda." He was beginning to feel on more solid ground now.

"What time did you leave the pub?"

"Ah left at half ten, had tae be up for a six o'clock start on Saturday morning," he replied.

"And you went straight home?"

"Ah stopped off at the chippy, it's halfway between the Tynecastle Arms and home. A fish supper is ma Friday night treat."

"I noticed that you're walking with a limp Mr Hughes, is

that permanent?" Lottie asked. This was the only thing this man had in common with their evidence so far.

"That? That's sciatica, it comes an' goes. It's the result o' drivin' a manual taxi for twelve hour shifts in a city full o' traffic lights - on an' off the clutch every two minutes," he explained, "Disnae half gie me gip fae time tae time. Funny, Ah wisnae really aware that Ah wis limpin'.".

Satisfied that Hughes could not have been on Holy Island the night the priest was killed, subject to his alibi checking out, Lottie eliminated Hughes from the enquiry.

"That's everything Mr Hughes, thank you for your cooperation, it's much appreciated," Lottie said, standing up.

"Ah can go now?" he asked, relief flooding through him.

"Yes, we'll have to get confirmation that you were at your local of course, but that's just routine."

He stood up, ready to leave and he hesitated before saying, "A' that stuff Ah told ye aboot when Ah was a boy ..." he said.

"Yes?" asked Lottie, puzzled.

"Ye dinnae have tae tell anybody, do you?" he looked from Lottie to Gary.

"I don't see any reason why I would have to do that Mr Hughes, but you might want to consider talking to someone about what happened to you," she replied.

"Ah'd like to, but Ah can hardly live on ma earnings after payin' child maintenance, let alone afford a counsellor," he said, shaking his head.

"There are a number of charitable organisations you could contact and, if you're not on the internet, Victim Support would be able to help you to get in touch with one of them. A few are specifically for men abused in childhood and I believe there is one for people who have been abused by priests."

Dean was very interested to hear this and made a mental note to go online at the first opportunity.

"Ah never knew that," said Hughes, "Ah might just do that." He shook hands with them both, all signs of antagonism and aggression gone now.

"Thank you," he said and left the interview room.

"Poor man!" Lottie said to Gary when he'd gone.

"Yes," said Gary, hoping he wasn't giving away any of his inner turmoil.

"Right, let's get Martin Davison in here next." she said.

19

A LITTLE WHILE LATER

L ottie and Gary discussed the investigation on the drive back to Berwick. As before, Gary had volunteered to do the driving so Lottie could think without having to concentrate on the road.

"What are we missing Gary? Hughes is obviously not our killer, so who the hell is?" she asked, exasperated.

"With any luck, Wright and Wheatfield might have come up with something while we've been away," he replied, rather flatly, his words at odds with his tone.

Lottie looked at him sharply and remembered his reaction while Hughes was telling them about how the priest's abuse of him had progressed.

"Is this case getting to you Gary?" she asked, tentatively.

"The case, the divorce, everything is getting to me boss," he replied bitterly. "We seem to be chasing our tails on this investigation."

Lottie was an intuitive woman and she wasn't convinced that it was their lack of progress in the investigation that was eating away at Gary. He'd been looking tired the past few days, as though he was losing sleep. There was definitely something about the interview with Hughes that had got to him. She tried to approach it sensitively.

"I couldn't help feeling sorry for Philip Hughes," she said, watching him for a reaction but his gaze remained steady on the A1 traffic.

"I can't imagine what his life must have been like, feeling special and guilty at the same time. The poor little lad must have been so confused, especially as he felt he couldn't even tell his parents." She shook her head sadly and added, "Well I'm glad he isn't our killer - his life has been bad enough without going to prison too."

Gary still said nothing, he just made a show of concentrating on the road, checking his mirrors, signalling and pulling out to overtake.

After a couple of minutes Lottie looked at him and said, "Gary did you not hear a word I've just said?"

His response was totally out of character for the usually easy going man and Lottie was shocked by it.

"For God's sake Lottie, can we leave the subject of Hughes and his pathetic life alone?"

They were coming up to a lay-by and, in her authoritative sergeant's voice, she said, "I want you to pull into this next lay-by Detective Constable Dean."

Gary checked his mirror, signalled and pulled into the lay-by.

"Turn the engine off please," she told him.

He did as he was told and sat staring out of the windscreen as the busy A1 traffic roared past, making the car rock slightly.

"Okay Gary," she said softly, "what's this all about? It's not about the way the case is going, is it?"

Still Gary said nothing, he was still staring ahead and his

hands clasped the steering wheel so tightly that his knuckles were white.

"Something Hughes said pushed a button Gary. I was aware of you freezing for some moments while you were taking notes." She continued in a gentle tone. "Did something like this happen to you too?"

Gary relaxed his rigid body, put his head in his hands and began to cry deep, wracking sobs. He was only vaguely aware of Lottie making soothing sounds. She didn't attempt to touch him, she just let him know she was there and he was grateful for that. Her training in domestic abuse stood her in good stead in these kind of situations.

Eventually his sobs subsided, he dried his tears and blew his nose. He looked at his senior officer and, with a wan smile, said, "There, you know my dark secret now. I've been having flashbacks since the start of this investigation and I really thought I had put the past behind me, but it was just waiting for something to come along and open the box again."

"Have you ever told anyone about this?" she asked.

"No, not even Shirley. I first had the flashbacks on our honeymoon. She was brought up a strict catholic and she refused to have sex before we got married." He looked at Lottie, incredulity in his eyes, "Can you believe that in the twenty-first century?"

"I suppose some people take their religion very seriously," she offered.

"Aye, but it suited me too. Ah steered clear of sex, I couldn't bring myself to experiment with the few girlfriends I had." He laughed mirthlessly, "No wonder they didn't last long ... until Shirley came along and she was as buttoned up sexually as me. It must have been luck that she conceived on our honeymoon because there hasn't been a lot of that in our marriage since."

Lottie let Gary talk. She felt that after years of suppressing this it was probably best to let him tell it in his own way and time.

"I've had depression on and off for years," he said looking at her and seeing her surprised expression, "but I kept it well hidden, only Shirley knew and, in the end, that was her excuse for telling me the marriage was over and that she wanted me to leave. I was devastated and begged her to give me another chance. I even suggested going for couple's therapy to help us." He looked at Lottie and said, "Do you know what she said to that?"

"What did she say?"

"She said it wasn't her who had the fucking problem, so why should she see a counsellor. There was no reasoning with her, so in the end I gave in and let her have it her way. I really miss the twins. Shirley makes it difficult for me to see them."

"Oh Gary, I'm so sorry," Lottie said, "and on top of all that there are the memories triggered by this investigation."

"That's not all," he said, feeling that since he was baring his soul to this woman, he might as well tell her everything. "She told me yesterday evening, just as I was about to drive home, that her boyfriend was moving in at the weekend." He told Lottie about the argument with Shirley the previous evening.

"Did you know she was in a relationship?" Lottie asked.

"Yes, but it's been going on for at least three years. She thought I didn't know, but it was obvious. All of a sudden she started wearing smart clothes and makeup to work, something she'd never done in all the years I'd known her, and she had late afternoon meetings to attend, she said, so the twins were left with her mother after school more and more."

He shook his head, "She must have thought I was daft enough to believe her lies, but really, I just kept quiet for the sake of the girls."

"And is the man friend definitely moving in at the weekend?" Lottie asked him.

"This case has made me hyper vigilant and feel even more protective towards Ellie and Poppy," he explained, "I think it was her telling me that a strange man was moving into my children's home and lives that made me see red. I lost it and told her I would push for the sale of the house if she moved him in and that I want better access to the children."

"What happened then?"

"I told her that we would communicate only through our solicitors from now on and I walked out."

"Hell Gary, poor you - on all levels I mean."

They sat in silence for some time, then Lottie asked, "Do you want to be taken off this investigation Gary?"

"No, I'll see it through. Besides," he added, "telling you about the abuse has lifted a heavy weight. I now feel like the black cloud that has been hanging over me since last Saturday has dissipated. When the case is solved I'll look into those organisations you were telling Hughes about. I'd never even heard of them." He turned to Lottie and smiled, "Thanks Sarge, you're a good boss and a great listener. Shall we get back on the road?"

"I suppose so, if you're sure you're up to driving the rest of the way."

"I am and I'll treat you to a stottie from Greggs when we get back," he said, "I don't know about you, but I'm starving."

20

BERWICK INCIDENT ROOM

L ottie and Gary got back to the office to the news that the DI had gone to the Diocesan Office in Edinburgh with a warrant authorising her to seize the personnel file of Fr Donovan.

"She's taken Jason with her," Gillian informed them, "he's as happy as a pig in shit, bless him."

"I'd like to see Fr Logan's face when she shows him the warrant," Gary said, "he was so arrogant when I spoke to him on the phone the other day."

"I'm hoping that all the complaints against Donovan will be documented, not just those of Hughes, McGuire and Davidson, which we already know about," said Lottie.

"In that case, there will be a lot of complaints that we will have to follow up on," Gary said, his heart sinking at the thought of more possible blind alleys.

Just then the internal phone rang and Lottie said, "I'll take it." One of the information handlers told her there was a member of the public who said he had important information about the murder and he wanted to speak to someone in authority.

"Put him through John," she said. She looked at the others and pointed to the receiver she was holding to indicate that this could be an important call.

"Detective Sergeant Lockhart speaking, how can I help you?" She sat in stunned silence as she listened to the caller. Gary and Gillian exchanged looks, wondering what was alarming the sergeant.

The voice at the other end of the line said, "You're not any closer to catching your killer, are you Detective Sergeant Lockhart?" the caller taunted "and I don't think you're going to catch him either."

"Who is this?" Lottie asked, rattled by the caller.

"That's for you to find out - if you can. Do you have anyone who's clever enough? I think not. It was quite a job getting the clothes off his dead weight," he chuckled. "Oh, by the way, did you like the calling card I left on the priest's chest? Bye for now Detective Sergeant Lockhart." And the line went dead.

"Shit!" she said, looking at the others, "that was our killer. Gary get that call traced, will you?" Gary went to his desk to set that in motion.

"What did he say Sarge?" Gillian asked, eyes like saucers.

"Well, he's an arrogant bugger," Lottie replied and she told Gillian and Gary, who'd returned, what the caller had said.

"How long until we know where the call came from Gary?" she asked.

"BT will have the information for us by later this afternoon."

"Okay, in the meantime, let's get on with confirming Hughes and Davidson's alibis for last Friday." she replied.

∼

DI CLELLAND and PC Wright arrived back in the office around three o'clock and Lottie put the kettle on to make tea and coffee for everyone.

Taking the mug of tea from Lottie, Clelland said, "Thanks Lottie, that's just what I need. I'm going to my office to go through these," she held up a box file containing the priest's personal record that she'd brought back from the Diocesan Office. I'm sure PC Wright will be more than happy to fill you in on our visit to Fr Logan."

"Before you go Ma'am," Lottie said, "we had an anonymous call earlier from our killer, taunting us because we haven't caught him yet and gloating that he's too clever for us."

Clelland stopped in her tracks. "Do you think it was a crank call Lottie?" she asked.

"No, he knew about what was on his chest and that the priest was naked."

"You've traced the call?" Clelland asked.

"It's being processed and we should have the information any time now," Lottie replied, checking the time on the clock on the wall.

"Okay, give me an hour to read this then we'll assess where we are," said the DI and she left the room.

"Jason are you going to tell us what happened in the Diocesan Office with the redoubtable Fr Logan?" Gillian asked, knowing he couldn't wait to tell them.

"Well!" he said, "he was not at all pleased to see us. At first the receptionist said we should have made an appointment as "Fr Logan is an extremely busy man." He put on a posh Edinburgh accent, "and the DI ..." Jason was almost gushing, "...she was magnificent. She told him that she didn't need an appointment as the warrant allowed her to access Fr Donovan's personnel file."

He took a gulp of his coffee and went on, "He - the receptionist - gave in and got Fr Logan who was really snotty, Ah mean *really*." He rolled his eyes heavenwards. "He was tall, bald an' as thin as a rake wi' glasses like the bottom o' beer bottles." He stopped for another drink of his coffee.

Lottie said, "Oh do get on with it Jason!"

"Right Boss," he said and continued with his story. "Fr Logan said he'd already told someone on the phone that he could not let us see Fr Donovan's confidential information. That, he said, looking down his long nose at the DI, can only be viewed by persons in authority in the Archdiocese." He imitated the Edinburgh accent once more and his small audience was enjoying his performance hugely.

"So then what happened Jace?" Gillian asked.

"The DI held up the warrant and she said - as calm as ye like - she said, "Fr Logan this warrant authorises me to remove Fr Donovan's personal information file" and she held out the warrant to him saying, "As you will see from the terms of the warrant, we are legally empowered to remove those documents. Refusal to cooperate on the Church's part, will put it in contempt of court with the inherent legal repercussions." That did it," Jason said, swallowing the last of his coffee, "ye should have seen his face, it looked like a balloon that a' the air had been let oot o'."

He sighed with pleasure at the memory of it. "And the score is," he said licking his finger and writing the number 'one' in the air: "DI Clelland 1, Fr Logan nil."

"That file will make interesting reading, I imagine," Dean said, looking at the door to the DI's office. "He sounded like he was hiding something when I spoke to him on the phone the other day."

"We'll find out soon enough, I'm sure," Lottie said.

Just then the phone rang and Gary answered it. When he came off he said, "That call was made from a pay phone at Haymarket Station in Edinburgh, they're emailing a digital copy over now."

"Good," replied Lottie, "get on to the station Gary and ask them to send over all their CCTV footage for the phone's location, see if we can spot the cocky bastard."

"Boss," Gary said and made the call.

21

THURSDAY'S BRIEFING

The Murder Investigation Team gathered around the white boards when DI Clelland entered the room.

"Okay everyone, we have a lot to get through so let's get started." She looked at Lottie, "Bring us up to date on the Hughes and Davidson interviews first Lottie, will you?"

"Ma'am," Lottie stood up and gave a detailed account of the interview with Philip Hughes. "We've checked with the taxi company and he was working from 6am to 6pm. His alibi at the Tynecastle Arms checks out too."

"So we can safely rule him out as our killer," Clelland said and she scored through his name on the white board. "What about Martin Davidson?"

"He was in Glasgow at a bank managers' conference during the day and stayed over at the hotel as a thank you from the bank to its valued employees, according to Davidson. The Royal Bank of Scotland has confirmed this, so he too is eliminated from our enquiries," she concluded.

"So, a jolly for the managers and us little people get next

to nothin' in interest fae our savins accounts," remarked PC Wright, "Ah've a good mind tae change banks."

"They're all the same Jace," replied Gillian, "they all look after their own, big bonuses at the end of the year while we're hammered with high mortgage rates and low returns on savings, that's if anyone can afford to save after paying the recent hike in mortgages."

Gillian had just suffered a huge increase in her mortgage repayments as her fixed term interest rate had just expired and, as a single parent, she was finding the current steep rise in the cost of living difficult.

DI Clelland looked at her in surprise but let it pass. Instead she said, "How are you getting on contacting the men on the list of choir boys PC Wheatfield?"

"It's very slow going Ma'am, leaving messages and waiting for people to get back to us. I've TIE'd about a third of them," she told her senior officer.

"Okay, I'll get HQ to organise a few bodies to help out with that. It's important we either get our killer from that list, or rule them all out."

"How did it go at the Diocesan Office Ma'am?" Lottie asked.

She smiled grimly and said, "Well I'm sure PC Wright has given you a blow by blow account, but I've been reading through Fr Donovan's personal information and it's clear that his superiors in the Catholic Church know what had taken place - not so much at the time, but retrospectively. There was a trickle of complaints earlier on, but once historical sexual abuse by priests, and other clergy, hit the news, increasing numbers of people wanted redress and compensation for what they'd experienced.

I can see why he ceased being the choir master around 2000," she said, looking at the notes she'd made when reading the Donovan file. "A prominent and devout member of the priest's parish discovered that his ten year old son was being abused by Fr Donovan and, rather than report it to the police, he went straight to the Archbishop. Donovan was told then that he would have no further access to children of either sex and he was ordered to undertake a period of therapy which, interestingly, was provided by the Catholic clergy. Keeping it in-house, as it were."

"It's so bloody wrong!" Dean interrupted. "The abuser got his therapy paid for by the church while poor Philip Hughes, who's struggling to make ends meet, can't afford counselling for the ongoing consequences of that man's abuse of him."

Lottie threw him a warning look and he stopped suddenly, going red from the neck up.

"Ah'm sorry Ma'am," he said, 'It's just that it's really unfair like."

"It's okay DC Dean," replied the DI, "child abuse, in all its manifestations, is an emotionally charged issue, especially for people who have children around the same age as those who were abused by Fr Donovan."

He nodded, grateful for the lifeline she had thrown him. He glanced at Lottie who now looked relieved that his outburst hadn't resulted in anyone being suspicious as to what may have triggered it.

"In terms of motive, there is no shortage of men who could bear a grudge against the priest and yet, so far, those men on the list that we've looked at closely, have been eliminated from the investigation." Clelland said. "Has the CCTV footage from Haymarket Station come in yet Gary?"

"Ma'am," he replied, "it came in just before we started the briefing. I think you should see it."

Gary went over to his computer and brought up the

footage. Everyone gathered around his desk as he played it. They watched as a man with a slight limp approached a bank of public telephones and made a call. One CCTV camera was directly above him but he kept his head down.

"Can you zoom in on him Gary?" the DI asked.

The man was wearing a hoodie with a baseball cap pulled low over his face, so all they could see was his nose and beard.

"Shit!" said Clelland, "go through all the footage Gary and see if we can get a clearer view of his face."

"Will do Ma'am."

They returned to their seats at the whiteboards and the DI stood deep in thought.

After some moments she said, "I think we can be sure that the man who spoke to DS Lockhart is the person who murdered Fr Donovan. The man in the footage has the uneven gait that Tim Lightfoot found in the evidence at the Priory and he knew about the word *PAEDOPHILE* on the victim's chest. That information was not made public, so only the killer could have known about it."

She sighed in exasperation. "You've all worked really hard, however we're almost a week in since the murder and we're no closer to identifying the killer. He's out there taunting us. What are we missing?"

"Ma'am," said Lottie, raising her hand, "what we're missing I think is a connection between the man in the CCTV and the priest. On the face of it, it looks like the priest was murdered as revenge by someone who had been abused by him in the past, but what if the killer wasn't? Which would explain why he hasn't shown up on our list of ex choir boys, as yet anyway. So there must be some other connection ... and possible motive for the murder."

"Ye-es," Clelland said, sounding doubtful, "I see what you mean, but what other connection? He is so bloody confident that he contacts us and goads us by making reference to the word *PAEDOPHILE* and he thinks he's so clever and has committed the *perfect murder* that he tells us we won't catch him."

"If I might suggest Ma'am," Lottie said, "Although said we needed to keep an open mind regarding motive, we have somehow become a bit blinkered by it all the same, which is what was worrying me last night. Perhaps we need to be thinking 'outside the box', as they say." She made quotation marks in the air.

"And do you have any ideas Detective Sergeant Lockhart?" Clelland asked.

"Well, I was wondering if we maybe showed our hand a little, so to speak," she ventured.

"Go on."

"If the DCI was to give a media statement along the lines of: we're looking for a person with an uneven gait, or limp and we believe the perpetrator was driving a silver 2008 Toyota Land Cruiser; and appeal to the public to come forward with any information which might help us etc etc."

The DI nodded slowly and said, "It's certainly worth a try and we have absolutely nothing to lose. I'll call him now. In the meantime, well done and follow up on what has come in so far. Lottie, you might want to read through the priest's personal file." She turned to go back to her office then stopped.

"Go home everyone and come back fresh in the morning. We'll meet at eight o'clock sharp."

It had been a very long day and nobody had to be told twice about leaving early. Lottie yawned and picked up her bag and jacket. "Night everyone, have a good evening." she said.

"Night Sarge," they replied as they left the room.

22

THURSDAY EVENING

Lottie

L ottie, who had been christened Charlotte Anne Lockhart and was born and raised in Edinburgh, had arrived in Northumberland in June 2008. She had managed, with the help of an old school friend, to escape from her abusive husband. She had simply waved goodbye to him one morning when she left for work and she hadn't returned home.

Instead, she had driven the eighty seven miles to her friend Kate's house, in Alnwick, with only the few essentials that she'd been squirrelling away, in her car, over the previous weeks.

Lottie had trained and qualified in therapeutic massage, much to her parents' disappointment and disapproval. They were both doctors and had expected Lottie to follow them into medicine. However Lottie, who had always been strong willed, followed her own choice of career and through that -

again to her parents' disapproval - she had met and married an abusive and controlling man called Denis McIvor.

Before their marriage Denis had shown no signs of being anything other than a devoted and loving boyfriend but he'd changed significantly just a short time after their honeymoon. He became possessive and extremely controlling and Lottie's attempts to regain her previous autonomy and strong will, against this controlling behaviour, had resulted in physical violence to make her tow the line.

After such violent attacks, he would apologise profusely and bring flowers. He would cry when he saw the bruises on her arms and body - he was careful not to hit her where it would show - and he'd tell her that he hadn't meant it and that it wouldn't happen again. Each time, she would believe how contrite he was and she would forgive him.

But, over time, his attentions became more oppressive. He would call her at work to make sure she was there and would often meet her after work, even though she had her own car. Keeping her car had been a hard won battle for her, but she'd convinced him that she needed it as she had to travel to different health facilities in the course of her day's work.

Very early on she thought his attentiveness was charming but that changed and she felt stifled, at times she felt like she was a prisoner in her own home. That was when his behaviour changed again.

He was no longer apologetic for the physical assaults on her, instead blaming her for what he said 'she'd made him do', by being stupid or recalcitrant. She would sometimes have to take time off work when her injuries could not be hidden by clothes or camouflaged by makeup.

Then one day she saw a poster in the ladies toilet at work. It asked,"Are you the victim of domestic violence and abuse?" and she stood for some time looking at it, the reality of her situation sinking in. By this time all contact with the world outside her marriage had shrivelled to nothing, apart from going to work.

The poster turned out to be a turning point in her life and she contacted her old friend, Kate Armitage, who she'd almost lost all contact with, by emailing her from her work computer. It was the one device that Denis did not have access to or control over. Kate sent her a pay-as-you-go phone and money to keep it topped up since, by this time, her husband had taken control of the joint finances and bank account.

She would never have told her parents about her predicament since they had made their feelings clear when she had gone ahead and married Denis against their advice. Relations between them were lukewarm, at best, and Lottie knew better than to approach them for help. She knew they would have told her that she'd 'made her bed' and now she must 'lie in it'.

Over a period of several weeks, with Kate's help and encouragement, Lottie collected a few possessions in an 'escape pack' which she kept hidden under the front passenger seat of her car, adding little items such as toothbrush, toiletries, underwear etc which she smuggled out of the house on her person.

Then, finally the day came when she left for work - at least that's where Denis thought she was going. Instead she drove to Alnwick where Kate was waiting to welcome her and help her to start a new life, free from the oppression and violence of her husband.

She had been in a state of fear when she reached Kate's house because Denis had been repeatedly trying to get her on her phone - which he had given her - and she had fifteen missed calls and several angry voice messages.

"What should I do Kate?" Lottie had asked, showing her phone to her friend.

"First of all, shut the damned thing down and later we'll have a lovely walk along the river Aln where you can toss it in and it'll be carried out to sea."

Lottie, who'd become a slave to Denis's calls, said, "Goodness, I'd never have thought of doing that."

Over time Lottie got some work in a private clinic and was able to afford a small flat in the town. She saw a psychotherapist over a lengthy period of time and she began to recover from the trauma of her husband's coercive and violent treatment.

She decided to have a total change of career and joined Northumbria Police, perhaps with a naive desire to help other victims of crime. She loved the work and the camaraderie of her fellow police officers and, after four years in uniform, she passed her detective's exam and became a detective constable.

In order to keep her whereabouts from her husband, Lottie had applied for a divorce through a solicitor in Edinburgh and on the twenty-fifth of June 2012 she received the piece of paper informing her that she was no longer legally attached to Denis McIvor.

WHEN SHE MADE it to detective sergeant, she relocated to Berwick Police Station and, by then, she was in a position to buy a little cottage of her own in the picturesque village of Norham where she had felt safe and had enjoyed life in the peaceful rural village. That is, until the disturbing events of the past week.

Tonight she had come home to find that a thick A5 size envelope had been put through her door. When she finally summoned the courage to open it, she was totally unprepared for its contents. There were photos of herself in various settings: going into the police station in Church Street; getting into her car in the car park; walking Dolly in the village and one of her going in through the front door of her cottage in Castle Street.

All of these images had been taken without her knowledge and she was shocked that she had been unaware of anyone taking them. She had ordered a CCTV doorbell but it wasn't due to be installed until early the following week.

Dolly stood in front of her stunned mistress and tapped her knee gently with her paw. "Oh Dolly!" she said, cuddling the hound, "this is going to have to stop. I'm going to report it first thing tomorrow."

In response and apparent approval, Dolly licked her face. "Come on," Lottie said, "let's go and get Jane and go for a walk. I need some fresh air and I'll feel safer if Jane is with us."

She left the photos on a side table and clipped Dolly's lead onto her collar and went to knock on Jane's door.

23

NORTHUMBERLAND POLICE HEADQUARTERS, NEWCASTLE

Thursday Evening

When DI Clelland made the phone call to her senior officer, DCI Flynn was not in the best of moods.

"We need to have a serious talk about this investigation DI Clelland," said Flynn. He usually called her Denise and she knew the conversation they were about to have would not be an easy one.

"But I'm not doing it over the phone." Denise Clelland's heart plummeted. "I want to see you in my office ASAP. Are you still in Berwick?" he barked the question.

"Yes Sir, but I'm leaving now." She grabbed her bag and coat and hurried out of the station.

For once the traffic on the A1 was moving well and she walked through the door of Headquarters at six twenty-five. After a brief visit to the ladies room to tidy herself up, she walked up the two flights of stairs to the DCI's office. She knocked on the door and waited.

"Come!" the voice inside said.

She rolled her eyes heavenwards, not for the first time wondering why he couldn't just say "come in", like normal people. She entered the room and stood while he finished reading a file on his otherwise empty desk.

As she waited, she glanced around the spartan-like room with its lack of personal touches and she thought that if she had the luxury of her own room here, she'd make it comfortable with a colourful rug and some soft lighting for working late into the evening. She was brought abruptly out of her reverie when Flynn snapped the file shut.

"This investigation into the priest's murder is not making the progress I had hoped for Detective Inspector Clelland," he began, as he sat with his elbows on the desk and fingers steepled, "especially from a high flyer like yourself."

DCI Gerald Flynn, Gerry to his intimates, was a small man in his late forties. He was going bald and his cold blue eyes held her in his gaze. He didn't care much for this woman who had entered the police service at the rank of DI, having come in on the graduate scheme. He mistrusted officers who had not come up through the ranks from the basic level of uniform, although he had to grudgingly admit that, so far, she had learned quickly on the job, and had the eye of the superintendent as someone who would go far.

Despite the adverse reflection on himself as Senior Investigating Officer (SIO), he was rather enjoying the way the investigation into the priest's murder appeared to be stalling.

"Are you any closer to identifying the priest's killer Detective Inspector?" he asked now. "The Super is being pressured by the ACC (Assistant Chief Constable) who happens to be a friend of Stephen Wright, the Roman Catholic Bishop of Hexham and Newcastle, and he wants the murderer apprehended and charged."

"Sir," replied Denise, "without making excuses, this has been a difficult case with a large pool of potential suspects. However, I believe we made a breakthrough today."

"How so?" he asked, raising his eyebrows and keeping his steely gaze on her.

"The man we now believe to be responsible for the murder of Fr Donovan called the office today and we managed to trace the call to a public call box in Edinburgh and we have CCTV footage of him making the call."

"And?"

"And we could see from the footage that his uneven gait corresponds to forensic evidence at the crime scene at Lindisfarne Priory. He also knew details of the victim's body that only the killer could know as these have not been made public."

"Have you now identified this man?" Flynn asked.

"Not yet sir, that's what I wanted to talk to you about. I believe if you made an appeal to the public with the new information regarding his limp and the silver Toyota Land Cruiser, it may bring us the response we need to be able to identify this man." she said, trying to keep any pleading from her voice.

He remained silent and she added with passion, "somebody out there must know something that will help us catch this man, even if they don't know it yet."

He sat in silence for some time, weighing up what she had said. On the one hand, he didn't want this bright young woman to succeed, but on the other, there was his own reputation to think of and there was always the pressure from above. It would not reflect well on the service if they were not seen to be doing everything in their power to apprehend the murderer of the defenceless old priest.

Eventually he said, "Very well, we shall give it one last shot Detective Inspector Clelland. I shall make a public appeal via the various media at ..." he looked at his watch " ... nine o'clock this evening. That should give the Press Office time to cobble something together."

He looked at her for some seconds and added, "If this does not lead directly to solving this case, it will be removed from you and handed to someone with more experience in the job. Understand?"

"Yes Sir, thank you Sir." she replied.

"That will be all," he said returning his attention once more to the file on his desk.

She left the room with a great sense of relief. "This has to lead us to the killer," she thought, "it just has to."

24

THURSDAY NIGHT

Edinburgh

"So, in conclusion, we are appealing for anyone who might have seen a tall bearded man, walking with a slight limp on Holy Island on Friday the fifteenth of September, that is Friday last; or a silver Toyota Land Cruiser with a 2008 registration anywhere on Holy Island that day from around midday to the early hours of Saturday morning, to please come forward and call our Crimestoppers number on 0800 555 111. Your anonymity is one hundred percent guaranteed. Thank you." said DCI Flynn, looking straight into the camera.

The man laughed and flicked the TV off, throwing the remote control down onto the sofa beside him.

"Do they think that's going to make any difference?" he asked the empty room, "how many people in the UK have one leg shorter than the other? Or, for that matter, how many people were on Holy Island that day, walking with a *slight* limp among hundreds - or even thousands - of tourists?"

He snorted. "They don't have a fuckin' clue. And as for the Toyota - who pays attention to one among hundreds of silver cars, especially with the registration plate obscured wi' mud?"

He got up and paced the room, a thrill of satisfaction flooding through him. "No, they're no match for me, they're looking for a bloody needle in a haystack, a fuckin' huge one at that." The man's arrogant confidence seemed to know no bounds.

∾

Norham

MEANWHILE, in Honey Bee Cottage, Lottie was on a FaceTime call with Frank. She hadn't seen him since Sunday, although they had exchanged numerous text messages.

"I'm sorry Frank," Lottie apologised for the third time, "we're at a crucial point in the investigation so I won't be free this weekend either."

"You always seem to be at a crucial point in something," he moaned. "If we lived together, at least Ah would see you when you got home or, if nothing else we could sleep in the same bed."

Lottie groaned inwardly and tried hard to keep her patience. "I know Frank, poor Dolly isn't sure whether she lives with me or Jane at the moment," she said, trying to lighten the conversation, but she could see the mulish expression appear across his face.

"Ah'm not a dog Lottie, Ah miss you and Ah really want

to spend time with you."

Lottie ignored his reference to Dolly and said, "Frank, I know my job puts a strain on our relationship, in terms of the hours I sometimes have to put in. I'm working on a serious crime, but in all fairness, you knew when we first started seeing each other that my job wouldn't always be nine until five, Monday to Friday. I have to be available when the work demands." Her voice was coaxing now, "Look, why don't you come up here tomorrow and I'll get home as early as I can? We could have a meal together eh?"

"Ah suppose so Pet," he said, sounding unconvinced.

"Stay over for the weekend, we can have breakfast together and you could walk Dolly along the riverbank, you know how much you both like that."

Frank sighed and realised that this was the most he was going to get. Lottie could see he was making an effort to pull himself into a more positive state of mind.

"I promise that when this case is solved we will spend a few days together, providing you can get time off, that is, alright?"

"Alright Lottie," he said, more cheerful now, knowing the last thing their relationship needed just now was for him to add more demands and pressure. "That'll be grand. Ah'll get there by six and take Dolly for a walk, then Ah'll prepare supper for when you get home."

"Great Frank, I'm looking forward to that," Lottie replied, glad that his awkward mood had passed. Dolly will be so happy to see you," she laughed, "She can hear your voice coming from my iPad and she's cocking her head from one side to the other wondering where you are."

"Ah'll see you tomorrow Dolly Girl," Frank said, he always called her Dolly Girl, and she wagged her tail happily.

"I'd best get to bed now Frank, tomorrow will be another busy day. Good night love, sleep well."

"Good night Lottie, I love you. See you tomorrow."

She tapped on the red 'end call' button and sighed. "Thank goodness he came out of that mood Dolly," she said, rubbing the hound's velvety ears, "I was beginning to lose my patience. What with a difficult case, a stalker and dead snakes through the door, I don't need Frank throwing wobblies."

In response, Dolly just groaned with the pleasure that Lottie's ear rubs always induced.

25

FRIDAY, 22ND SEPTEMBER

BERWICK INCIDENT ROOM

Since the appeal the previous night, calls had been coming in from the public with numerous reports of sightings of men with a limp and silver 4x4 vehicles, only a few of which were Toyota Land Cruisers.

Police constables and civilian staff had been drafted in from other stations to help handle the volume of calls. DI Clelland gathered the team together just before lunch-time to brief them.

"As you know, the public appeal by DCI Flynn last night has resulted in a lot of calls to the Crimestoppers line and extra staff have been brought in and are working their way through messages that were left overnight, as well as answering the live calls coming in now."

She looked at the solemn faces of her team. They all knew they were struggling to make a breakthrough in the case and they feared that she was about to tell them that the investigation was being handed over to another team.

"While most of the calls are from people who believe they have some valuable information for us, others are just time wasters. Fortunately they are in the minority and the experienced call handlers are adept at weeding them out.

So far, we have several reports of sightings of a man, or maybe more than one man with a limp on Holy Island last Friday, and several sightings of silver 4x4 vehicles, although none have been clearly identified as a 2008 Toyota Land Cruiser," she said, sounding weary, "and, as yet, we have had no reports of a silver Toyota Land Cruiser *and* a man with a limp together."

Lottie raised her hand and asked, "How did your talk with the DCI go last night Ma'am? I mean, we all saw the appeal but we're all wondering whether we are being kept on the investigation or if it's being handed to another team." She had just voiced what the other team members had been thinking and worrying about.

Clelland shuddered inwardly at the memory of her encounter with the SIO and said, "Last night I had a meeting with DCI Flynn in person and he, in no uncertain terms, expressed his dissatisfaction with the way the investigation is going."

"Does he ken how many choir boys we've got on that list?" PC Wright asked with indignation.

"Yes, PC Wright," Clelland replied, "he knows exactly how many. However, he is under pressure from the ACC who apparently is a close friend of the Catholic Bishop of Hexham and Newcastle and the Bishop wants the priest's murderer caught and charged."

"Aye, don't we all? Ah dinnae suppose the Bish realises just how hard we're workin' or how many potential suspects there has been, given how long the priest had boys under his dubious care?" Wright spoke out again. "Ah mean, we've been workin' our blo ... eh socks off Ma'am, wi' a' due respect."

While PC Wheatfield glared at the outspoken young Scotsman, Clelland was trying to stop a smile curving her lips. She cleared her throat and said, "No, PC Wright, I don't think he does and I don't think he cares." She looked at Gillian now.

"PC Wheatfield, you've been coordinating the extra help on completing the enquiries re the list of ex choir boys, can you give us an update on how that's going please?"

"Yes Ma'am, everyone on the list has now been traced, interviewed and eliminated from our investigation. I'm afraid that line of enquiry has turned out to be a dead end," she reported.

"But a necessary line of enquiry nevertheless," added the DI, "and the situation now with regard to us, as a team continuing on this investigation, is dependent on whether an arrest results from the appeal made by DCI Flynn last night." There was a communal groan around the room.

"We have until midnight on Monday to identify, find and bring our killer into custody," she told them.

"So no pressure then," said Wright glumly. He had been so excited to be a member of this murder investigation team and he knew how hard everyone had worked, but he now felt they had been walking blind all along.

"Exactly Jason," replied Clelland, with sympathy, "no mean feat."

Just as she was about to end the briefing a civilian officer knocked on the open door and stood with a piece of paper in her hand, waiting for the opportunity to speak.

"Yes?" Clelland asked.

"Ma'am" the woman said, a little nervous to be interrupting a team briefing, "I've just received this message from a member of the public." She walked over and handed it to the DI.

"Thank you," Clelland replied, nodding for the woman to go. As she read the message her face brightened and the team waited in anticipation.

"Apparently a Tesco delivery driver's vehicle was almost hit by a silver Toyota Land Cruiser on Holy Island last Friday afternoon. This is his phone number," she said, handing the slip of paper to Lottie, "Give him a call and ask him if he can describe the driver of the Toyota."

"Ma'am," Lottie said going to make the call.

"Everyone else carry on with what you were doing and we'll meet back here at ..." she looked at her watch, "five o'clock for the final briefing of the day."

They returned to their desks, their emotions a mixture of despondency and hope: despondency because of the deadline; and hope that the Tesco driver's information might bring them closer to their, as yet elusive, killer.

26

THAT AFTERNOON

Lottie called the number of the delivery driver but it went to voicemail. Frustrated, she left a brief message asking him to call her back, leaving the number of her direct line.

"I'm going out to get a sandwich, does anyone want anything?" she asked the others.

Gillian said, "No thanks Sarge, I can't afford to buy lunch these days, I've brought a sandwich with me and I'll make do with the office instant coffee."

"Can ye get me a Bridie and a diet coke please?" Jason asked, handing over a five pound note.

"Do they sell Bridies down here?" Gillian asked, wrinkling her nose in distaste. A Bridie, properly known as a Forfar Bridie, is a Scottish 'delicacy' of minced beef, and onion in pastry.

"Well, if they havenae any Bridies a sausage roll will do," he replied.

Lottie took the money and said, "I see you're still on a healthy diet Jason," then she asked Gary if he wanted anything.

"No thanks, I've brought a roll in and I'll have instant coffee too."

"Okay, if the Tesco man calls, tell him I'll be back soon," Lottie said and she grabbed her bag and hurried out of the office.

Lottie had just finished lunch when her desk phone rang. It was the Tesco delivery driver.

"Hello, DS Lockhart speaking," she said, then she took her notepad and pen, ready to write down his information.

"Hello," the voice replied.

"She looked at the name on the scrap of paper the DI had given her and said, "Mr Inglis, I believe you have some information for us regarding the appeal last night?" She hoped that this was the lead they so desperately needed and her heart was beating faster with anticipation.

"Aye," he replied, in a broad Scottish accent, "it wis ma last delivery for the one tae two o'clock slot an' Ah wis in a bit o' a hurry because Ah needed tae get back tae the mainland before the causeway was cut off by the tide at five to two," he continued almost without taking breath, "an' Ah had tae be in Belford for the two tae three o'clock deliveries, ye see."

"And you saw a silver Toyota Land Cruiser on Holy Island, Mr Inglis?" Lottie interrupted quickly.

"Aye, that's right hen an' ye can call me Billy," he replied, not minding the interruption to his stream of consciousness.

"Can you tell me exactly what happened and what you saw Mr ... eh, Billy?" she asked, looking across to Gary and shrugging her shoulders, perplexed.

"Well, Ah wis jist turning intae St Cuthbert's Square for ma last delivery on the island when this maniac came roond the corner oan the wrong side o' the road. Ah had tae slam oan the brakes an' the food crates in the back o' the van were shuntin' intae one another like, an' it wis only when Ah got tae Belford that Ah discovered Mrs Wilson's eggs were totally smashed up. Anyway ... now, where was Ah?" he paused.

"You were telling me about the car almost crashing head on with your van Billy," Lottie said, trying not to grind her teeth. "What make of car was it?" she asked again just to make sure they were talking about the same vehicle.

"Oh aye, it wis a silver Toyota Land Cruiser, a 2008 reg an' Ah would've went after him if Ah hadnae been in such a hurry." he told Lottie.

"Did you get a look at the driver of the Toyota Billy?" Lottie asked, crossing her fingers, now that Billy seemed to be getting to the point.

"Aye, he wis a big guy wi' a mop o' dark curly hair an' a beard."

"Would you be able to recognise him again, do you think?"

"Aye, but Ah can dae better than that, ma dash cam caught the whole thing. Tesco had them installed in case o' accidents, but between you an' me hen, Ah think it's tae keep tabs oan us as well."

"Excellent Billy!" Lottie said, while everyone else on the room looked at her expectantly.

"Can you send it over as soon as possible please?" Lottie asked.

"Ah'm no' workin' the day but Ah'll phone the office an' ask them tae dae it Sergeant Lockhart." he offered.

"Would you ask them to send it right away Billy, it's very urgent."

"Aye, nae bother hen, cheerio."

"Thank you for your help Billy, we really appreciate it,"

she said and she smiled as she put the receiver back on its cradle.

"Well?" Dean asked for everyone, waiting to hear about the other end of the conversation.

"He was a bit of a sweetie wife but, it looks like our killer almost had a head on collision with Mr Inglis van and his dash cam recorded the whole thing."

"Fantastic!" cried Wright, punching the air.

"We'll still have to identify him so don't get too carried away Jason," she cautioned, "although he did say he had a beard, like our man at Haymarket Station."

"But it's the closest we've been able to place the killer to the murder scene, right in St Cuthbert's Square," Dean said.

"I'm away to tell the DI," said Lottie, walking with a spring in her step for the first time in days.

Her phone was ringing when she got back and she quickly picked it up. "DS Lockhart," she said, then after listening to the voice at the other end, her face fell and she said, "I see, well thank you for letting me know."

"Oh no," Gary said, "another set back?"

"You could say that Gary," she replied glumly, "that was the Tesco home delivery office telling me they delete the dash cam recordings every four days."

Everyone in the room fell silent at this latest blow.

AT THE FIVE o'clock briefing Lottie broke it to DI Clelland about the dash cam footage and she was at a loss to understand why the DI was still smiling.

"Don't worry about that," she told the team, "our technical guys will be able to retrieve it. It'll take a little while longer but we'll get it back. Isn't modern technology wonderful?" she smiled beneficently at them, believing that they might have just broken through the deadlock.

"DS Lockhart, get back onto Tesco and arrange for one of our tech team to get that dash cam. Once they've got it back at the lab they should be able to retrieve the footage," she said, then added, "emphasise the urgency and tell them we need it by tomorrow at the latest.

"Ma'am," Lottie replied and hurried to make the call.

"In the meantime everyone, go home and enjoy your Friday night - but not too much," she added, looking at Jason, "and be back here at eight thirty tomorrow morning."

"Ma'am," they chorused and quickly shut down their computers and left.

27

HONEY BEE COTTAGE

FRIDAY EVENING

I t was only five-thirty when Lottie got home and she was pleasantly surprised, as she hadn't been home this early in a couple of weeks. Dolly met her in the hallway and was almost beside herself with happiness to see her mistress. After fussing over her for a few minutes, Lottie took off her jacket and put the kettle on.

She had called Jane before leaving work to let her know that she would be home early enough to give Dolly her dinner.

"Time for a wee before dinner Dolly," Lottie said, opening the kitchen door for her to go out into the back garden, then she set about getting food ready for her.

Dolly was still snuffling around the garden when Lottie tapped the dish with a spoon, the signal to Dolly that her food was ready. She trotted into the kitchen, tail wagging in anticipation, as Lottie put the dish down on the raised feeding station, made specially for greyhounds, as the floor is a long way down for a large hound.

Lottie made herself a cup of tea while Dolly ate, then decided she had time to have a quick shower before Frank arrived. She hurried into the bathroom, taking her tea with her.

She had just dressed in trousers and a long sweater when she heard Frank turn the key in the front door and she went into the hallway to greet him, behind an ecstatic Dolly.

Lottie smiled as she watched the mutual adoration between her beloved Dolly and her boyfriend. "How are you Dolly Girl?" Frank said, rubbing her ears.

Frank, in his turn, was surprised and delighted to see Lottie there, he'd thought she wouldn't be home for another hour, at least.

"You"re home!" he exclaimed, grinning widely, "that's champion, we can make supper together."

"Yes love," Lottie replied, "we all got away early so let's make the most of the evening together, shall we? Starting with a leisurely walk along the riverbank."

On hearing the word 'walk' Dolly got excited and bounced about the hallway until the attachment of lead to collar kept her bouncing in just one spot.

"Ah'll just leave ma stuff in the bedroom and change into ma walking boots Lottie," Frank said, removing the overnight bag which still hung on his shoulder. While Frank was doing that Lottie took her walking jacket from the hook in the vestibule and slipped into her wellies.

It was a beautiful early autumn evening with the fragrance of turning foliage, alongside smoke from wood burning stoves in cottages throughout the village.

Frank and Lottie chatted companionably as they walked along hand in hand, while Dolly trotted ahead, busying herself with the scents left by other dogs and riverside creatures.

"How's the investigation going now Pet?" Frank asked, "It must be about a week since the murder eh?"

"Oh don't remind me about the length of time," Lottie replied in mock despair, "although we might be getting somewhere in identifying the killer. But let's leave my work back in the office, eh love? How has your week been Frank?"

So they chatted about current affairs and Newcastle United's chances in the Premier League this year, as they turned at the end of the walkway and made their way home again.

When they got back to the cottage Frank went into the kitchen to make a start on the meal while Lottie lit the fire in the sitting room so it would be cosy later. Dolly, pleasantly tired after her walk, sprawled on the sofa, happy that the fire had been lit.

Frank was busy chopping vegetables for his signature dish of pasta and sauted vegetables and Lottie put plates in the oven to warm.

"Would you like white or red wine?" she asked, "there's an Australian Chardonnay chilling in the fridge or I can open a bottle of Shiraz if you'd prefer that?"

"Shiraz for me please," he replied, as he scooped the vegetables into the hot olive oil in the wok.

Lottie opened the bottle and poured them both a glass. She put Frank's on the counter next to the hob.

"Cheers" she said, as she took a sip of the fragrant, dark red liquid.

Frank laid down the spatula and picked up his glass, "Cheers, to a lovely evening!" and he clinked his glass against Lottie's.

Lottie set the table while Frank cooked the pasta and made a salad. They moved smoothly around each other in the kitchen like a well rehearsed dance and she thought that having Frank moving in might not be such a bad idea after all, especially after the kind of week she'd had.

It was dark by the time they sat down to eat and Lottie had lit candles and dimmed the central light, creating an intimate mood.

Afterward, they took their wine into the sitting room where the fire had warmed the room against the chill of the late evening. Dolly was now stretched out on the rug in front of the fire and Lottie and Frank snuggled up on the sofa.

She sighed deeply, enjoying the relaxation and the warmth of Frank next to her. "This is lovely," she said, "it's so good to sit here with you and just relax and not worry about anything."

"Mm," Frank murmured, "it's lovely to be here in our own little bubble of warmth and love." He stroked her cheek and kissed her. "Let's go to bed," he said and pulled her gently to her feet, leaving Dolly snoring in front of the fire.

28

NORHAM

S he heard the footsteps behind her again and, this time, they were gaining on her. She tried to quicken her pace but she felt like she was wading through deep sand and her legs felt so heavy she could hardly lift one foot in front of the other.

Just as she put the key into the lock and had pushed Dolly in ahead of her, she felt his breath on the back of her neck.

"I've got you now," he said, "I've waited a long time Lottie, but I've got you now."

She felt his hands on her throat and she panicked. She knew she was going to die if she didn't do something now. With a supreme effort she threw herself back against him as hard as she could in an attempt to unbalance him and get away. She could hear Dolly whimpering on the other side of the front door. Then she woke up.

"Lottie, Lottie," It was Frank, "wake up Pet, you're havin' a nightmare."

She was breathing hard and her heart was thudding against her ribcage. A worried looking Dolly stood at the side of the bed, whimpering and trying to lick her face. She sat up and soothed the distressed hound, then she said, "Oh Frank, it seemed so real. I thought he was going to strangle me, I thought I was going to die."

"Sh, sh," Frank soothed, putting his arms around her, "ye're alright now, it was just a bad dream Pet."

She took some deep breaths to calm herself, stroking Dolly's head all the while. "But that's just it Frank, it's not just a bad dream, it's real."

She told him about feeling she was being followed and the figure following her and Dolly earlier in the week. Then she told him about the dead snake and the photos she'd been sent.

Frank was shocked and asked, "Did you report this to the police?"

"I had the police out when I found the snake, but I've been so busy with work that I haven't had the chance to report the photos. I'm getting CCTV fitted on both outside doors in a few days time, so I'll feel safer then," she said and added, "Please don't fuss Frank, I'm fine now."

He looked at her closely and saw that she did seem to be back to her usual composed self. "I'll make us a cuppa," he said, "put your dressing gown on and keep warm."

A few minutes later she was sitting on the sofa cradling a mug of tea to warm her chilled hands despite the warmth in the room. Frank had stirred the embers into life and Dolly was once more stretched out in front of the fire.

As she sat there, the niggle that had been at the back of her mind since Monday shifted focus, and now sat squarely within her conscious mind.

She carefully laid her mug of tea on the end table in case her shaking hands spilled it. A chill like ice water flooded through her and she began to breathe erratically. She was back there again, frozen to the spot in terror, his hands gripped tightly around her throat. He was so close, spittle hit her face as he said, "Don't even try to get away Lottie. You can run but you can't hide forever." This was not a dream, this was a memory.

"Lottie, what is it?" Frank's urgent voice brought her back to the present. "What is it Pet?" he asked again.

"Oh Frank," she said, her hand at her throat protectively. "I know now who it is. I know who has been following me, it's *him*."

In the years since she'd escaped from the vile, psychopathic Denis McIvor, she'd never spoken his name and had referred to her ex husband only as *him*.

"He's tracked me down after all these years," she shook her head in disbelief. "I don't know how on earth he did, but he has. I knew there was something about the figure on Monday night that bothered me and it's been niggling away at the back of my mind until now and that dream." She lifted the mug of tea from the table and sipped it as she began to feel calmer.

"He's been trying to scare you Lottie, Ah don't know if he intends to harm you after all this time, but he's definitely playing mind games with you," Frank said, then added, "but Ah do think you should report everything to the police, let them trace him and warn him off."

"You're probably right Frank, and I think all this happening on top of the stress of the investigation has me overwrought," she agreed. "I'm over what he did to me and his controlling games, I worked through it years ago in therapy. Playing with my mind was always one of his favourite tools."

"He no longer holds any power over you Lottie, unless you let him," Frank reminded her.

"I know Frank," she said, stroking his cheek lovingly, "and I won't let him disturb another minute of my sleep." Now that she knew who the stalker was, the threat had lost its power.

She stood up and held her hand out to Frank, "Come on, let's get back to bed, I'm going to be up again in four and a half hours."

29

SATURDAY, 23RD SEPTEMBER

L ottie arrived in the office just after eight o'clock and was surprised to see that Gary was already there. Frank had said he would take Dolly for her early walk so Lottie could concentrate on herself and get into work early.

She'd slept surprisingly well after they'd gone back to bed and Frank's solicitousness made her feel very close to him. Despite the nightmare and disturbed night, she felt very positive this morning.

"Good morning Gary," she said, "you're in early."

"Aye, I didn't sleep well, tossed and turned most of the night, so I thought I might as well get up and make a start on anything that's come in overnight." He yawned widely.

"I'm glad I've got you to myself before the others come in Gary, as I wanted to talk to you about my stalker." She took the photos out of her bag and handed them to him. "I know for certain now that I'm not imaging it, take a look at these."

He looked at the photos and let out a low whistle. "That's really creepy Lottie, and you weren't aware of him taking these?"

"No, just the strong feeling that someone was watching me and of being followed on Monday night." She also told him about the dead snake and her nightmare last night and the realisation that it had been her ex husband who had managed to track her down after more than a decade.

She thought about it for some moments, then said, "I don't even know if I would recognise him now, he could have changed a lot in fifteen years, I mean a fifty year old man might look very different from when he was thirty-five. He could be bald and wear glasses, or whatever. He might even have deliberately changed his appearance, disguised himself so I wouldn't notice him in a crowd."

"I suppose so," Gary agreed.

"Appearance is one thing but it was the way the person on Monday night walked that had niggled away at me all week."

"Are you going to report him?" Gary asked.

"Yes, if I can get a minute today, I'll go downstairs and report everything. They already have my statement about the snake incident. I should let them have these photos too, as evidence," she said, putting the photos back in her bag.

Gary looked at the clock, "Go now," he urged, "I'll let the DI know you're reporting a serious incident."

Lottie hesitated for a moment, then nodded her head. She picked up her bag and went downstairs to the main office.

By the time she returned to the incident room the rest of the team were busy with calls or looking at their computer screens.

"The DI wants to see you Sarge," Gary informed her, "how did you get on downstairs?"

"Fine," she replied, they took a statement and are going to check him out. They'll get back to me."

She knocked on the open door of the DI's room, which was euphemistically named 'office' but was the size of a broom cupboard. Clelland looked up and said, "Come in Lottie and close the door."

She asked Lottie about the 'serious incident' that Gary had mentioned and Lottie gave her a succinct account of the events of the past week.

Clelland looked at her appraisingly and asked, "Are you alright? I mean do you feel fit and alert enough to continue on this investigation?"

"I'm fine Ma'am, especially now I've realised who it is and it's now in the hands of the police and out of my mind." Then she added, "I feel better now than I have all week."

Clelland nodded, reassured, "Very well, that's all."

When she got back to her desk Gary said, "That was the tech guys on the phone for you, they've retrieved the Tesco dash cam footage and are sending it over to you," he nodded towards her computer and said, "it should be there now."

"Thanks Gary," she said and logged onto her computer. After just a couple of minutes she got up and went straight to Clelland's office to let her know. A few minutes later the team was gathered around Lottie's desk viewing the dash cam recording.

The footage showed the Toyota Land Cruiser coming around a corner on the wrong side of the road and coming to an emergency stop. The driver thumped his hand on the steering wheel and shouted something, jabbing his forefinger angrily towards the Tesco driver. He then reversed and shot off past the Tesco van.

"Rewind it a bit Lottie," Clelland said, and, as Lottie did, she exclaimed, "there, freeze it there! Zoom in on his face!"

"Aye," said PC Wright, "there's nae doubt about it, that's

the same person in the CCTV footage at Haymarket Station."

"Yes, but who the hell is he?" asked Clelland. They were all silent, looking at the computer screen when Gary's phone rang with a ring that indicated it was an internal call. Gary picked it up, then looked at Lottie, holding his hand over the mouthpiece.

"It's Dr McGuire wanting to speak to you Sarge, he said he saw Thursday's appeal and thinks he has some new information."

Clelland said, "Okay everyone, we've seen enough of the video for now. Let's leave DS Lockhart to take this call."

"Hello Dr McGuire," Lottie said, "you think may have some new information for us?"

"Maybe," he replied, sounding unsure, "I don't want to sound like a crank caller, but I saw the appeal on Thursday night and ..." he paused.

"And you've thought of someone it might be?" Lottie prompted.

"Well I didn't think much about it at first but there was something at the back of my mind, you know, like a half-forgotten memory you can't quite grasp?"

"And now?" Lottie encouraged, wishing the man would get on with it.

"And this morning, the memory came back to me." He paused to get thoughts straight in his mind, then said, "It's probably a long shot, but I remembered there used to a lad waiting outside the church for his brother after choir practice and he had a bit of a limp, I think he had one leg shorter than the other."

"You know who this boy is?" she urged.

"It was the boy's brother who was in the choir, his name was Michael Kelly and he had a twin brother called

Anthony. They were identical apart from Anthony having this permanent limp," he paused, "Well, that and the fact that they were nothing alike personality-wise. Michael was a quiet gentle boy whereas Anthony was what you'd call a 'bruiser'."

Lottie searched through the papers on her desk for her copy of the list of former choir boys and ran her finger down it looking for Michael Kelly.

"Michael Kelly is deceased," she said to McGuire, her heart sinking again after a surge of hope.

"Yes, about ten years ago," replied McGuire sadly. "He took his own life after suffering years of mental illness. Seems like the poor boy never got over Fr Donovan's abuse."

"Do you know where Anthony lives?" Lottie asked.

"I'm sorry, I have no idea Detective Sergeant Lockhart, I just heard about Michael's death from an old friend a while afterwards. Apparently it was reported in the Edinburgh Evening News at the time. I don't know if his parents are still alive. It's a long shot, as I said, but I thought I should let you know."

"Yes, thank you Dr McGuire, I'm very grateful to you for this information." She hung up and saw that the team had been listening to her end of the conversation and were very curious to hear what Dr McGuire had told her.

30

SATURDAY AFTERNOON

After Lottie had told the team about her phone conversation with Dr McGuire, there was a murmur of excitement as they gathered in front of the murder boards. Philip Hughes and Brendan McMahon had been cleaned off the board since Hughes had been eliminated as a person of interest and Police Scotland were investigating McMahon.

The DI wrote Anthony Kelly at the top of the board now, as their prime suspect.

"So, to summarise what we now know, given this new piece of information: Michael Kelly, who is on our list as deceased, was one of Fr Donovan's choir boys at the same time as Hughes, McGuire and Davidson. He had an identical twin brother ..." she pointed to the board, "Anthony, who according to Dr McGuire, walked with a limp. Also, according to Dr McGuire, Michael committed suicide some ten years ago, after years of suffering from mental illness."

She paused, "DC Dean, I want you to look up the article McGuire said was in the Edinburgh Evening News, see what other information you can glean from it."

"Ma'am," replied Dean, noting it down.

"Michael Kelly had ongoing mental health problems, we assume as a result of being sexually abused by Fr Donovan when he was a choir boy. Then Michael, after years of illness takes his own life and his twin brother, Anthony, decides to take matters into his own hands and murders Donovan as retribution for losing his brother."

"But why wait ten years to do it?" asked PC Wheatfield, "I'd have thought if he was that angry with the priest he'd have sought him out right away and killed him."

"We probably won't know the answer to that until we find him. What we do know is that Fr Donovan's murder was premeditated and it was carefully carried out, to the extent of hanging him in what is regarded as a holy place." replied the DI. "We need to find this man and we need to find him as soon as possible. At the moment, all we have is a name and a date of birth - get that from the list, will you DS Lockhart?"

She then turned to PCs Wright and Wheatfield. "You two try to trace him through DVLA, HMRC, the DWP and the Edinburgh phone book. Split the various agencies between you, we have a deadline to meet remember."

"Ma'am" Lottie raised her hand.

"Yes, DS Lockhart?"

"Well I hate to burst your bubble now we've had this breakthrough, but we won't be able to contact HMRC, DVLA or the DWP until Monday," Lottie said, apologetically.

"Shit! I'd forgotten it's the weekend," replied Clelland, clearly dismayed. "Well you'll just have to make sure you're on the phone at 8am on Monday morning. Check the phone book in the meantime and Catholic Churches in Edinburgh, although I doubt he's a member of the church given what happened to his brother."

"Ma'am, Ma'am," PC Wright had his hand up and he was almost jumping up and down with excitement."

"What is it PC Wright?" she asked.

"I've just googled the DVLA and their lines are open until two o'clock on a Saturday."

Everyone checked their watches, it was now one-thirty.

"Okay Jason, call them and let's hope you're not at the end of a long queue of callers."

There was a flurry of activity as the team members set about their individual tasks.

Gary found the article mentioned by Dr McGuire. It appeared in the Edinburgh Evening News on Wednesday 18th September 2013. It read:

"HEARTBROKEN MUM PAYS TRIBUTE TO GENTLE SON

Mrs Theresa Kelly, mother of 37 year old Michael Kelly, paid tribute to her son who tragically died at the weekend. Michael was found hanged in his family home on Sunday afternoon and the police believe the cause of death to be suicide which they expect will be confirmed by the coroner.

Mrs Kelly said, "Michael had always been such a kind and gentle boy who always put the needs of others before his own and he did a lot for charity He used to sing at a local care home where he was loved by the residents and he helped out at the Cat and Dog Home in Seafield on Saturdays."

She went on sadly, "He had suffered from depression on and off for years, since he was a teenager, but just recently I thought he'd turned a corner and he seemed much better and more able to deal with life. He'd been put on new medication and we thought he was finally on something that was making a difference. That's why this came as such a shock, totally out of the blue. I mean, I might have expected it a few years ago when he was in the darkest depths of depression, but not now. I'm only glad his poor Daddy wasn't alive to suffer this tragedy."

Michael leaves behind his twin brother, Anthony, who was too upset to give a statement."

GARY MADE copies of the article and distributed them to the team.

At five past two Jason put down the phone and shouted, "Got him!" He was waving a piece of paper in his hand with the address he had just been given by the DVLA. "Of course, they insisted on calling the station here to verify who I am, Ah mean, Ah could've been anybody like."

"Well are you going to share this information with the rest of us or are you going to keep it to yourself PC Wright?" asked Clelland who had just walked into the room in time to hear him.

"Aye Ma'am, Anthony Kelly registered a vehicle at the following address: 14/6 Murrayburn Gardens, Edinburgh."

"Thank you Jason, let me have that piece of paper and I'll liaise with Police Scotland and ask them to pick him up and take him to the local police station."

Half an hour later Clelland's phone rang. It was the police in Edinburgh informing her that Kelly was no longer living at that address. Neighbours told them that he hadn't lived there for the last three years, at least. Apparently he left there just before Covid and none of them knew where he had moved to.

When she informed the team, the mood in the room seemed to deflate instantly.

"Keep on with the phone book in the meantime and start contacting people on the list again, someone might just know where he's living now."

She looked at their glum faces and, forcing herself to sound more cheerful than she felt, she added, "we're further on today than we were this time yesterday, so do't give up hope."

"Ma'am?" Gary said, raising his hand.

"Yes?"

"I've put a copy of the Edinburgh Evening News article on everyone's desk, but I just wanted to draw your attention to something."

"And what's that Gary?"

"Michael Kelly took his own life on the 15th September 2013 and Fr Donovan was murdered on the 15th September ten years later. I think that's significant."

31

HONEY BEE COTTAGE

SATURDAY EVENING

When Lottie got home around six o'clock there was a delicious aroma coming from the kitchen. She took her jacket off and fussed over the welcoming performance Dolly was giving, then went into the kitchen.

"What's for supper?" she asked, "it smells delicious."

Frank, who was wearing a striped apron, kissed her lightly on the lips and poured her a glass of wine that had been 'breathing' on the worktop. Handing it to her, he said, "Vegetable lasagne, garlic bread and a Greek salad."

"Mm, I could get used to this," Lottie replied, taking a sip of her wine. She leaned against the worktop and asked, "How was your day?"

"Oh we had a champion day, didn't we Dolly girl?" he said to the hound who was lying in the doorway between the kitchen and sitting room so as not to miss any scraps that might fall to the floor from the counter. "We had a long walk on the far side of the river and Dolly had a veritable feast for her senses - I think there must have been badgers and foxes along the path during the night," he smiled, "she was in her element."

"How was your day Pet?" he asked.

"It was interesting," she said, thinking back to her meeting with the station sergeant before she came home. "Have I got time for a quick shower?"

"Aye Pet," Frank replied, looking at the timer on the cooker, "supper will be ready in twenty minutes."

"Great! I'll tell you about my day over supper." She put her glass on the counter and went to the bathroom.

While they ate, Lottie told Frank about reporting the other incidents involving her ex husband to the police, and about what Sergeant Appleby had found when he had done a search on him.

"Actually Frank, I was shocked to hear that he'd been in prison for ten years and he was only recently released, just a few months ago, in fact." Lottie reported.

"Ten years is a long sentence, especially since they usually only serve just over half of it if they behave themselves," Frank said, wondering what he had been gaoled for.

"Yes, it is," Lottie replied, reflectively, "He was convicted of rape and a brutal attack on the woman he was living with." She shuddered, "Poor woman! Apparently neighbours reported hearing a woman's screams and called 999. Thank God they did since he might have killed her otherwise."

Frank put his hand over Lottie's, "You're okay Pet, you got away."

"I did, but he obviously became a lot more violent after I left him. Maybe he was punishing her for me leaving him, maybe he punished every woman he met after I left?"

She paused and looked up, alarmed. "I'm wondering if this changes things Frank."

"How do ye mean Pet?" he asked, concerned at her anxious expression.

"Well, just yesterday I said that I had worked through the fear and trauma in therapy, and now I find out he nearly killed a woman and has served a long prison sentence for it. Do you think he's coming after me now? He obviously knows where I live."

"You've officially reported a crime now, so what did the sergeant say?" Frank asked.

"He said he'd make sure a patrol car came past my cottage every hour until they track him down and warn him off. He'll keep me informed."

"Look Lottie, Ah know what you said last Sunday, but why don't Ah stay here until the problem with *him* is sorted?"

Lottie bit her bottom lip, always a sign of inner turmoil, swithering whether to grab Frank's offer - which is what her instinct was telling her to do - or whether that would give him the wrong signal.

As if reading her thoughts, he said, "Ah won't take it as an invitation to stay for ever, honestly," he squeezed her hand and smiled affectionately. "I love you Lottie and I want you to be safe - that's all for the time being. Otherwise, I will honour the agreement we made in Giovanni's on Sunday."

She was relenting, and said, "But what about your work Frank? It's a long commute every day."

"That's not a problem, besides I have a few days annual leave booked this coming week and it won't be forever - just until the police issue him with an injunction, or whatever it's called, to keep him at a safe distance from you."

Lottie smiled and gave a huge sigh of relief. "Thank you Frank, you're a lovely, caring and kind man and I'm very lucky to have you."

She thought for several moments then said, "I feel like a great weight has been lifted from me. I think it must have been stressing me more than I realised."

"Do you fancy watching a film?" he asked.

"Yes," she replied, gathering up their supper dishes. "Let's leave these to soak in the sink and we'll find something funny and light hearted."

"What about *Four Weddings and a Funeral*? I haven't seen that for ages."

"Perfect. I don't have to be in work until nine-thirty tomorrow, that's the DI's concession to it being Sunday." She smiled, feeling truly happy for the first time in over a week. "Come on," she said, taking his hand and leading him into the sitting room.

32

MORPETH

SATURDAY EVENING

While Lottie and Frank were enjoying an intimate evening together, Gary Dean sat alone in his little flat in Morpeth, brooding.

He was in a dark place and he wasn't sure if he could extricate himself from it. He wandered aimlessly around the small flat and found himself in the tiny kitchen. He took a bottle of beer from the fridge, opened it and went back into the living room and drank it straight from the bottle, it was his third since coming home.

He wouldn't usually have more than one, especially when he had work next day, but he'd stopped off at Morrison's on his way home, to pick up a microwave meal and he'd thought, "What the hell? I could do with a drink."

He felt that the murder investigation was teetering on the brink of failing to catch the killer. The fact that they had a name for the man and what an advance in the case that was, did not penetrate the depths of his despondency.

In addition to, and perhaps because of the murder, he was having increasingly disturbing flashbacks from the abuse he'd suffered as an altar boy. He knew it was wrong but he couldn't help feeling that the priest had got what he deserved.

"Fucking bastards, the lot of them!" he shouted out loud to the empty room, "They all deserve to be hanged."

Then, on top of all that, today was the day that Shirley's fancy man was moving in with her and his daughters. He checked the time on his watch, it was only eight-thirty and they wouldn't be in bed yet. He desperately wanted to talk to his daughters. He hesitated for all of sixty seconds then dialled the land line number.

It rang for what seemed like a long time and he was about to hang up when it was answered.

"Hello," the voice said and Gary sighed with relief. It was one of the girls and not their mother, as he had feared it might be.

"Poppy?" he said, it's Daddy.

"I'm Ellie Daddy," she said giggling.

"You both sound so alike on the phone sweetheart," he tried to sound upbeat. "How are you and what did you do today?"

"I'm okay. Poppy and me went to Grandma's today because Mummy was helping Joules to bring his stuff here and we got a takeaway for dinner because Mummy said she was too tired to cook." Ellie prattled on, totally unaware of the pain in her father's heart that her words were causing.

"And how do you feel about Joules coming to live with you Ellie?" he asked, feeling uncontrollably jealous.

"It's okay Daddy," she said. "He's got a guitar and he's going to teach me and Poppy how to play it. Isn't that cool?" she said, excitedly.

"Yes sweetie," he managed, his heart felt like it was being squeezed in a vice. "Can you put Poppy on now?"

He heard the receiver clatter on the hall table as Ellie

called upstairs. "Poppy, it's Daddy! He wants to speak to you."

Just then Shirley came out of the lounge and picked up the handset. "What the hell do you think you're playing at Gary?" she said through gritted teeth.

"I'm speaking to my children," he replied, "since you've made it impossible for me to have them here, the only option I have left is to talk to them on the phone."

"You're doing this deliberately, aren't you, because you know Joules was moving in today?" she said angrily.

"Mum, I want to speak to daddy!" He could hear Poppy's plaintive voice in the background.

"Well you can't," she told the child, "go to your room!" He could hear Poppy's cries of protest. "And you go to hell," she said to Gary, banging down the receiver and cutting him off.

"You fucking bitch!" he said to the dialling tone and he put his head in his hands and wept. He wept for himself, for his children and for the mess his life had turned into.

"How did it come to this?" he asked the empty room, "One minute I have a family and a normal life and the next minute I have nothing, fuck all."

He sat for a long time, reflecting on everything that was wrong in his life and wondered, "What's the point of it all? Who would miss me if I wasn't here?"

He supposed Ellie and Poppy might miss him but his access to them was getting less and less, thanks to Shirley, and they seemed to be getting used to life without him. Shirley, he reckoned, would be only too pleased if he was completely out of the way, then the house wouldn't have to be sold and she could go on living the way she wanted without any disruption.

This last thought galvanised him and brought him

sharply out of the suicidal path his thoughts had begun to go down. "Fuck you Shirley!" he said vehemently, "you're going to have to compromise. You're *not* getting the house to yourself and your lover, not without me getting my share."

The dark, heavy cloud that had been hovering over him for days began to lift and he felt he could see a way ahead. It wouldn't be easy, he knew that, but there was now the slightest glimmer of hope in his heart.

He thought about the organisations that Lottie had spoken about earlier in the week, then he started to google them on his phone and wrote down the contact details.

When the investigation was concluded, and he now felt that it would be, over the coming days, he would contact Victim Support and get the help he needed to deal with the trauma of the past. He knew making that contact would be just the first step on what was sure to be a long and, probably painful, process of recovery.

He felt exhausted now and he knew he would sleep tonight. He got up slowly from the settee, put the empty beer bottles in the recycling box and went to bed with the hope that tomorrow would be a better day.

33

SUNDAY 24TH SEPTEMBER

BERWICK POLICE STATION

I t was two o'clock and the mood in the incident room in Berwick Police Station was sombre. The searches for Anthony Kelly in the phone book, and talking to men on the choir boy list had been exhausted and had produced no new information on Kelly's whereabouts.

It was Day 9 of the investigation and the Murder Investigation Team had been working without a day off. They had until midnight the next day to make an arrest or else the case would be ignominiously taken out of their hands.

Even the usually chic DI Clelland was looking drawn and her shiny bob hairstyle was looking a bit flat and tired. She had gathered the team together and tried to lift their flagging spirits. She stood in front of the murder boards and spoke to them.

"Okay, we have drawn a blank on trying to find Kelly's whereabouts from today's search, but please," she looked earnestly at the assembled faces, "please don't be down-hearted as we have two main sources that will be available to us first thing tomorrow that we could not access today - HMRC and the DWP."

She wrote these on the whiteboard. "If he is in paid employment then the Inland Revenue will have up to date details for him. If not, unless he is independently wealthy, the Department for Work and Pensions should have him on their system."

"What about a final appeal to the public Ma'am?" Lottie asked, "after all he's someone's workmate or neighbour, or even husband or boyfriend."

"Unless he's living like a hermit," Wright said dejectedly. For once Jason's enthusiasm failed him and everyone looked at him in surprise.

"What?" he said defensively, "Ah'm just sayin'."

Lottie continued, "Since the appeal on Thursday night by DCI Flynn, we now have a name, a motive and a description … as well as the limp and the dash cam photo which is quite clear."

They all looked at the enlarged image from the Tesco van's dash cam and, Lottie now fired up said, "Dark hair, going grey at the temples, blue eyes and a black beard threaded with grey. Add a limp and his name and somebody out there has to know where he is."

The DI, whose thought processes had become lethargic, gave herself a mental shake and said, "You're right DS Lockhart! I'm going to run this by DCI Flynn and the Press Office can hopefully get something out in the media this evening."

The SIO approved the proposed new media release. All the information and images on Kelly were sent to Northumbria Police Press Office to be prepared and released as a statement and public appeal on all major networks, including internet news sites, that evening.

Since it was now a matter of waiting for government offices to open on Monday morning and the results from the evening appeal, DI Clelland sent the team home early.

"Go home and be back here, ready to go at eight o'clock sharp tomorrow morning."

"Yes Ma'am," they said enthusiastically and gathered their belongings, glad to be out of the office on such a fine day.

"Do you fancy going for a drink Lottie?" Gary asked as they went down the stairs.

"Why not? Just the one and then I'll have to get back for Dolly's tea and walk."

They sat in a quiet corner of the pub around the corner from the station and Gary told her about his abortive phone call to his daughters the previous night and Shirley cutting him off before he had the chance to speak to Poppy.

"I feel really jealous, you know Lottie, they seem to have accepted that man into their lives so easily. I feel like I've been replaced and they're all excited because he says he's going to teach them to play the guitar."

He shook his head sadly, "What can I offer them, eh? Bugger all and she won't even let them stay over because my flat isn't suitable," he made quotation marks in the air, "for an overnight stay."

Lottie put her hand on his arm and said, "I'm sure you've not been replaced in their affections, or otherwise, Gary. You're their Dad and when the divorce comes through and the finances are settled, you'll be able to get a place suitable to have them at weekends or overnight." She smiled encouragingly and added, "and can you see the guitar lessons lasting? The twins will probably get fed up, or he will."

"Yeah, you're right," he said, smiling, "bairns don't stick at any one thing for long at their age. Thanks Lottie, I feel better now I've talked about it, rather than let it go round and round in my head like I do when I'm on my own." He took a sip of his beer and added, "I would have phoned my sister last night but she's on holiday in the Algarve."

"Nice for some," said Lottie, finishing her wine spritzer.

"Yeah, Marjory never did take to Shirley, said she was 'all fur coat and no knickers'. She thought she was in a class above our family."

Lottie let out a peal of laughter, "God, it's a long time since I heard that phrase Gary. That's what folk used to say about posh people who lived in Morningside which is an affluent area in Edinburgh."

Gary drank the last of his half-pint and they got up and left. As they approached their cars Lottie said, "Let's see what tomorrow brings Gary. I think we're getting closer to arresting our killer. I have a feeling that either the appeal, or the early morning call to the government bodies, will turn up something and lead us to his door."

34

SUNDAY AFTERNOON
EDINBURGH

"Come away in Tony, Ah'll make us a pot o' tea, the kettle's just boiled," said Mrs McLaren when she opened the door to Anthony Kelly. He was in the habit of getting her weekly shopping on a Sunday from the nearby Aldi supermarket.

He followed her down the narrow lobby into the kitchen where he laid the shopping bags on the floor out of the way, so the arthritic old woman wouldn't trip over them.

"Ah'll put them away for you later Mrs McLaren," he said and sniffed, appreciatively. "Is that fruit scones Ah can smell?"

She paused in the middle of pouring the boiling water over the tea bags in the warmed pot and asked, "Would ye like a couple wi' yer tea son?"

She knew the answer, as this was a weekly ritual after he had brought her shopping home. He liked to help out his old neighbour by getting what she called her 'messages', and she liked to offer him tea and home baking on his return.

She set a tray with the cups, saucers, teapot, milk jug and

sugar bowl and said, "You take them through tae the livin'
room while Ah see tae yer scones ... butter and jam, as usual
son?"

"Aye, that would be smashin' Mrs McLaren," Anthony
replied, lifting the laden tray and taking it through to the
front room.

In the living room she laid the plate of scones on the
coffee table in front of the settee where Anthony was sitting
and she sat in her own raised armchair by the gas fire.

"Are you no' havin' anything tae eat Mrs McLaren?" he
asked, thinking that the old woman had been getting
thinner this past month or so. He hoped she wasn't ill,
although she was her usual cheery self.

"Naw, Ah'm no' hungry Tony, Ah had ma dinner no' that
long ago." Most working class people in Scotland called
their midday meal 'dinner' and the meal at five or six o'clock
their 'tea'. "An' Ah keep tellin' ye tae call me Elsie, son, no'
Mrs McLaren," she added.

"Oh Ah couldnae dae that Mrs McLaren, ma mother
taught me tae address older ladies as Mrs whatever," he
informed her. "It wouldnae be respectful to call ye by yer
first name."

She smiled fondly at him. "Ye're a good laddie Tony an'
yer mother would be proud o' ye, God rest her soul," she
added, making the sign of the cross. Mrs McLaren was a
devout Catholic, although her arthritis meant she didn't
always get to weekly mass.

That was the one thing Anthony wouldn't help her with.
When she'd asked him to walk her to mass on a Sunday, he
had point-blank refused. Without going into detail, he had
tried to explain, as gently as he could, that he blamed the
Catholic Church for the death of his twin brother. The old
lady had accepted this with equanimity, knowing that his

mother hadn't lived long after his brother's death. Died of a broken heart, she thought. She just made her own, slow way to St Cuthbert's, which was only a few hundred yards along the road, when her arthritic knees weren't too painful.

Mrs McLaren lived on the ground floor flat of the tenement in Slateford Road and Anthony had found her lying in the stair after a fall, not long after he had moved there some three years ago and a firm friendship had ensued between them.

"How's work goin'? she asked.

"It's fine," he told her polishing off the last scone, "it's no' sae bad in this weather but Ah'm no' lookin' forward tae the winter, it can be gey cauld on frosty mornins." Anthony worked in the Roads Department of Edinburgh City Council, so he was outside in all weathers.

"Aye, Ah imagine it would be son. But ye'll get wrapped up well an' wear thae big industrial boots tae keep yer feet warm an' dry," she said, solicitously.

"Aye, a wooly hat an' gloves as well," he smiled at her.

"Could ye go another scone Tony?" she asked, trying to delay his departure, as he took the receipt and change for her shopping out of his pocket and handed it to her.

"No thanks, Mrs McLaren. Ah'll have tae get goin' and get ma claes ready for work the morn, an' Ah havenae hoovered or tidied up much this week, so Ah better see tae that as well."

"Tut, tut," the old lady said, in mock disapproval, "what ye need is a nice wife tae look after the hoose for ye, wash an' iron yer claes an' have a hot meal ready for ye comin' hame fae work." At eighty-five, Mrs McLaren was of the old school and believed men and women had separate roles and lives in society.

Anthony laughed and said, "Ah think Ah'm a bit long in

the tooth for that now Mrs McLaren, an' a wummin would jist cramp ma style."

Mrs McLaren laughed too, "Aye, Ah suppose so, what are you young folk like, eh?" Then she added, as usual, "Thanks for gettin' ma messages son, Ah dinnae ken what Ah'd dae withoot ye."

"It's ma pleasure," he said, adding, "Ah'll see masel' oot, you jist sit where ye are."

"Cheery- bye son," she called as he shut the front door.

35

MONDAY 25TH SEPTEMBER

MIT ROOM, BERWICK

Early Monday Morning

The incident room in Berwick Police Station was a hive of activity at 8am on Monday morning.

On Sunday night Northumbria Police Press Office had released the photo of Anthony Kelly, along with his name, and physical description They had asked for anyone who knew this man, or his whereabouts, to contact the police on their Crimestoppers line. By this time, the news of Fr Donovan's murder the previous weekend was widely known and reported in the media.

Numerous messages had been recorded the previous evening from people claiming to know Kelly, leaving information on where he lived and worked. Some were obviously hoax calls, but there were those who claimed to be his neighbours and people he worked with.

The team divided the calls between them and, by eight-twenty they had ascertained that Anthony Kelly lived in a top floor flat at 100 Slateford Road, Edinburgh and that he was employed by Edinburgh City Council, as a labourer working in the roads department. At the same time, this intelligence was confirmed by the Inland Revenue.

When DI Clelland entered the room, the excited buzz of conversation and speculation was at such a volume that she had to shout to get the attention of her team. They quickly informed her about Kelly's address and workplace.

"DS Lockhart, call the Roads Department and find out exactly where he's working today." She checked her watch, "He's almost certainly at work by now. When we have that information we can send uniforms to pick him up there."

"Will do Ma'am," she replied and picked up the phone.

Three minutes later, she said, "Ma'am, he didn't show up for work today which, apparently, is unusual for him."

"Damn!" she replied, "I suppose there was always the risk that the press release would alert him and that he might go to ground."

She doubted her own judgement, not for the first time in this investigation. "Okay, I'll arrange for local uniforms to go to his address and see if he's there, but I wouldn't hold my breath." She sighed and shaking her head said, "This investigation seems to have been doomed from the start."

"Do you think we should have a surveillance team watching the building where he lives Ma'am?" suggested Lottie, "As well as the airport, train and bus stations, that is if he hasn't already left the city."

"Yes. I'll get onto the local police right away. Dean alert British Transport Police. Lottie you contact security at the airport."

She went into her little office to contact the local police in Edinburgh which was her first priority. Then she would have to inform DCI Flynn at HQ and she wasn't looking forward to the prospect of that. She could see any future promotion going up in smoke already.

DCI Flynn was enraged, as she had guessed he would be. "Well, that's just great Detective Inspector Clelland," he said down the phone in a dangerously calm voice. "I had my doubts about that media release - letting the killer know we're coming to get him."

"With all due respect Sir," replied Clelland, "you did authorise the release."

His response was a low, barely audible growl. These days senior officers did not shout at their junior members of staff, except in trashy TV dramas.

After a short silence, he asked, "What measures have you put in place Detective Inspector?"

When she gave him the details, he replied, "Very well, keep me informed, but bear in mind, our killer could be travelling by car, take care of that, will you?" he said and hung up.

36

EARLY MONDAY MORNING
SLATEFORD ROAD, EDINBURGH

As Anthony Kelly stepped down onto the ground floor landing of the tenement building, the door to Mrs McLaren's flat was quickly opened, as though she had been waiting behind the door for him.

He looked at her in surprise as she stood there in her dressing gown, beckoning to him and, in a hoarse whisper, she urged him inside.

He was alarmed, thinking the old woman had taken ill during the night, but he was even more alarmed when he heard what she had to tell him. She led him into the kitchen in case they would be heard from the communal stair.

"What's wrong Mrs McLaren? Are ye ill?" he asked, concern showing in his kind blue eyes.

"No," she replied quickly, "did ye no' see the news last night?"

He hadn't bothered to watch the news since Thursday night's appeal, so he said, "Naw, Ah cannae be bothered wi' the telly some nights an' Ah wis readin' a good book. What's so urgent aboot last night's news?" Then the first frisson of alarm swept through him.

"The polis wanted tae ken where an Anthony Kelly lived. They said they wanted tae speak tae him urgently in connection wi' the murder o' thon priest on Holy Island."

She was speaking quickly and quietly and he strained to hear what she was saying. She continued, "They said they wanted tae eliminate him fae their enquiries like. They gave a description that matched you Tony." She looked directly into his eyes, worry - or was it fear? - clearly etched on her old wrinkled face.

"Tell me it wisnae you son, ye're such a good and kind laddie, ye couldnae be capable o' doin' anything like that, could ye?" She was wringing her hands anxiously now, unable to believe the laddie, as she thought of him and was so fond of, could be a killer.

He took her gnarled, arthritic old hands in his and looked her straight in the eye, "Of course it wisnae me Mrs McLaren, Ah wis here when the priest was murdered. Don't ye remember? Ah cut yer grass an' trimmed the hedge for ye last weekend, besides, Ah widnae dae anything like that," he lied, looking straight into her eyes.

"Aye, that's right son, so ye did," she replied, looking greatly relieved.

"Now if that's a' it wis that ye wanted, Ah have tae get tae work," he looked at his watch, "an' Ah've already missed the ten past eight bus."

"A'right Tony, sorry tae have kept ye back son," she said apologetically, "See yersel' oot, will ye? Ah'm jist gonnae put the kettle on."

"Aye, nae worries Mrs McLaren," he replied, hurrying along the lobby and letting himself out. But instead of leaving the tenement, he ran up the stairs, taking them two at a time, and bolted into his flat in a blind panic.

Why hadn't he kept tabs on where those incompetent

cops were in the investigation? And how the fuck did they know his name? He felt like things were unravelling and he needed to be in control again. He berated himself as he pulled a holdall from the top of his wardrobe onto the bed and started flinging clothes into it.

He grabbed his toothbrush and toothpaste in the bathroom, then caught sight of his face in the mirror. Mrs McLaren had said the description had matched him. "How the fuck do they know what Ah look like?" he asked his reflection.

He grabbed scissors from the cabinet above the sink and hastily began cutting at his beard, until big clumps of it lay in the sink. He then plugged in the electric razor that hadn't been used in over a year, and shaved around his mouth and chin, as closely as he could in his hurry.

"That'll have to do," he said to the mirror, feeling the stubble rasp against his work-hardened fingers.

He went into the drawer in his bedside cabinet and took out his wallet and passport. "Thank God I remembered to shave," he thought, as he didn't have a beard in his passport photo.

Lastly, he tore out of his orange, and very conspicuous, work overalls and boots and quickly donned jeans and a jumper, then hurriedly put on a pair of trainers.

He cautiously opened the door to his flat and quietly hurried down the stairs with his small travel bag. He had £50 in his wallet which he thought should be enough for a taxi and he'd get money from a cash machine later. He headed out into the street.

By sheer luck, a black taxi was heading into town with its 'for hire' light on and he waved it down.

"Where to?" asked the driver.

"Airport, as fast as you can, Ah'm runnin' late."

"Nae probs," replied the driver and he did a quick U-turn to the outrage and blasting of horns of the traffic going in both directions.

37

A SHORT TIME LATER

On receiving the request from DI Clelland, local police were dispatched to Slateford Road to arrest Anthony Kelly on suspicion of murder.

The stair door was operated by a buzzer system and, as there was no answer from Kelly's buzzer, they buzzed the ground floor flat, hoping somebody was in the building to let them in.

"Hallo?" Mrs McLaren said.

"It's the police Ma'am, can you let us in please?" the officer said.

Mrs McLaren was standing at her open door when the two officers, a man and a woman, entered the building but they hurried past her and up the two flights of stairs towards the top landing.

"If you're looking for Tony Kelly, he's no' in, he's away tae work," she called up after them.

They carried on, without acknowledging her, and she could hear them banging on Tony's door. The commotion had brought someone on the middle floor out onto the landing to see what was happening.

"What's goin' on Mrs McLaren?" the woman called down, leaning over the bannister, but Mrs McLaren only shrugged her shoulders, wondering now if Tony had been telling her the truth earlier.

"Mr Kelly, Police, open up!" she could hear the officer call as he rattled the letter box.

On the top landing, the female officer had crouched down to look through the letterbox. "He's either not in, or he's not going to answer the door," she said to her partner. "Get the enforcer out of the car Graham."

A couple of minutes later, the door was forced open and the officers entered the flat warily.

Graham said, "You check the rooms at the end of the hallway Janine, and I'll check the ones at this end."

A minute later Graham called to Janine from the bathroom. "Come and see this!" They both looked at the clumps of hair lying in the bathroom sink.

"Looks like our man tried to change his appearance," observed Janine, "and he was obviously in a hurry since he didn't bother to clean up the sink after him."

"I'll radio it in and the controller can pass this information on to Berwick, they'll need to be on the lookout for someone without a beard now."

"I'll talk to the neighbours," Janine said and left the flat.

The neighbour on the middle landing, a Mrs Brown, wasn't able to tell her anything other than that Kelly had lived there for around three years and that he worked for the council.

Mrs McLaren had gone back into her flat and put the kettle on. She was feeling confused and hurt and she needed a cup of tea. She was sure the police would come to her door at any minute.

She had just sat down in her chair by the fire when the

doorbell rang. She put her cup on the side table and walked wearily and painfully to the door. It was the female officer who stood there, followed by the man she had buzzed into the tenement.

"Come in," she said in a resigned tone and she led them into the living room.

"We just want to ask you a few questions about your neighbour on the top floor Mrs ?"

"Mrs McLaren," she told them, and Janine took out her notebook and pen and started taking notes.

"How well do you know Mr Anthony Kelly?" The male officer asked.

"Tony's a good lad," she told them, "he's awfy good tae me. He goes for ma messages and looks after the garden. What dae the polis want wi' him?"

He didn't answer her question but asked, "Mrs McLaren, when did you last see Mr Kelly?"

"Ah saw him goin' oot tae work this mornin' aboot the back o' eight o'clock," she told him, "He leaves at the same time every mornin'."

She felt torn between helping the police and protecting Tony, even though he may have lied to her. What's he supposed tae have done?" she persisted, "Ah mean ye dinnae brek doon people's doors for nothin'."

"We just need to talk to Mr Kelly in connection with an incident last weekend," he said, not wanting to frighten the old lady by mentioning the word 'murder'.

"Does Mr Kelly have a car?"

"Naw, he was hurrying tae catch his bus, he gets the number 34 to work, an' ye can take it fae me son," Mrs McLaren told him, "Tony wouldn'ae hurt a fly, he's a good, carin' an' helpful neighbour."

The two officers exchanged glances, knowing they

weren't going to get any more useful information from the old woman, and they stood up."

Janine put her notebook away and handed a card to Mrs McLaren, "Thank you for your help Mrs McLaren, if you remember anything else, or if Mr Kelly returns, please give us a call on that number."

"Aye, Ah'll dae that," she said, knowing she would do no such thing.

She saw the officers to the door and then went into the kitchen and put the card in the bin.

38

MONDAY MORNING
BERWICK INCIDENT ROOM

The information gathered by the uniformed officers at Kelly's flat had been passed on to DI Clelland and she was much relieved that the headache of searching for Kelly escaping by car had been ruled out.

She spoke to the team. "According to the officers who were dispatched to Kelly's home, a neighbour reported seeing him leave for work just after eight o'clock. We know that he didn't go to work but the time he left home is probably reliable. DC Dean, can you ask British Transport Police in Edinburgh to check CCTV footage from 8am this morning and let them know that Kelly has shaved his beard off, so the photo they have is out of date. Everything else is the same, it's just the beard that isn't there."

"Will do Ma'am."

"DS Lockhart, will you let security at Edinburgh Airport know about the change in his description. They'll need to alert all the airlines and check-in operators. Also ask them to check their footage from 8am on too."

"Ma'am," Lottie replied.

"It's just a matter of waiting now," Clelland told them,

"It's in the hands of the Edinburgh police, there's no point in us going up there, he could be anywhere in or out of the UK, if he's already managed to leave Edinburgh by rail, bus or air."

There was a tense atmosphere as Gary and Lottie liaised with British Transport Police and airport security. They all felt powerless, onlookers waiting for the situation to unfold.

With some trepidation, Clelland went to her office to update DCI Flynn.

39

EDINBURGH AIRPORT

I t was eight-forty five when the taxi drew up at the terminal of Edinburgh Airport and the driver stopped the meter.

"That'll be twenty-five pounds please Sir," the driver said, turning in his seat to the partition window.

Kelly handed him thirty pounds and waited for his change. He took the five pound note and got out of the taxi, much to the driver's disappointment, his hopes of a tip gone. "Mean bastard!" he said as he pulled away and put on his 'for hire' light again.

During the journey he'd tried to engage his passenger in conversation, but Kelly had given monosyllabic responses and looked out of the window, discouraging any further interaction.

Kelly entered the terminal building and stood looking around him, not knowing which way to go. He had twenty-five pounds in cash and he decided that would be enough for the time he would be there and he could pay for anything else by credit card.

He was still feeling rattled by what Mrs McLaren had

told him and he sat down in a nearby waiting area to calm himself and gather his thoughts.

They'd be looking for a man with a beard and he congratulated himself that he'd shaved it off. "That should buy me some time," he thought to himself. He had no way of knowing that the police were already in possession of this fact.

He looked around the airport, pretending to people-watch but all the while he was checking for police or security guards and trying to work out his next move.

He approached a departures board and he saw that there was an EasyJet flight to Malaga due to leave at 10.45 "That should give me enough time to buy a ticket and get through the security checks," he thought.

It had been years since he had been out of the UK but his passport was still valid for another three years. He went to the EasyJet desk and enquired about a seat on the 10.45 to Malaga.

"I'm sorry Sir," the sales assistant said, checking her computer screen, "that flight is full, but bear with me a minute and I'll see if I can get you on another flight today."

She typed on the keyboard and clicked the mouse a few times, then smiled widely at him. "I can book you on our 10.30 to Gatwick and there's a seat available on the 1300 hours flight from there to Malaga." She looked at him enquiringly, "Shall I book you onto those flights?"

He paused, trying to make up his mind and she added, looking at her screen, "The seats are selling fast on the onward flight Sir."

That made the decision for him, at least he'd be out of Edinburgh soon. "Yes, thanks."

"Do you have any baggage to check in?

"No, just carry on," he pointed to the floor where his holdall lay. She gave him a flight tag to attach to it.

"That comes to £235 altogether, including airport taxes," she said, "How would you like to pay Sir?"

He handed her his credit card and punched in his PIN. "Thank you Sir. May I see your passport please?" She took it from him, gave it a cursory glance and handed it back to him along with his boarding pass and said, "Thank you Mr Kelly. You'll be boarding at Gate 3 in fifty minutes, have a pleasant flight."

He breathed a huge sigh of relief as he left the desk to mingle with the crowds queuing up to check in. In his naivety he gave no thought to the many CCTV cameras around the terminal building, both inside and out.

40

BERWICK INCIDENT ROOM 09.45

D ean came off the phone call to British Transport Police in Edinburgh and reported to DI Clelland that there had been no sighting of Kelly between eight o'clock and nine-thirty, but they were keeping a lookout for anyone matching his updated description. Lottie approached as Dean was leaving the DI's office.

"Ma'am," she said, sounding excited, "I've just had a call from Security at Edinburgh Airport. Their CCTV at the terminal entrance picked up a man matching Kelly's description getting out of a taxi at eight forty-seven. He was heading into the terminal building."

Clelland was already lifting her phone to inform the police station close to Edinburgh Airport but Lottie hadn't finished and she put it down again.

"Security there have been very efficient, they know we want to talk to Kelly in connection with a murder ..."

"Yes, go on," Clelland said impatiently.

"Ma'am," Lottie said apologetically, "another camera caught him at the EasyJet sales desk where it was confirmed that he'd bought tickets for flights to Gatwick and then on to Malaga from there."

"What are the flight times?" Clelland almost barked the question.

Lottie checked her notes, "The 10.30 Edinburgh to Gatwick and the 13.00 from Gatwick to Malaga. They're sending the CCTV footage to us now."

Clelland snatched up the phone again and signalled for Lottie to stay put. She called the police station by Edinburgh Airport and succinctly told them Northumbria Police needed them to apprehend Kelly before his flight left at 10.30. "I'll have the suspect's photo and description sent to you immediately." She ended the call.

"They're dispatching cars now. Thank God the station is only two minutes from the terminal building."

She turned to Lottie, "They've allocated an officer to stay on the line who will be in radio contact with the team they've dispatched and they will keep us informed of what's happening as it happens. They're also alerting the airport authority about this operation. If it all goes to plan, they'll arrest Kelly either before he boards or when he's on board awaiting take off." She stopped to draw breath and then added, "Keep the team informed, will you?"

"Yes Ma'am," Lottie said and turned to leave.

"Oh and tell Dean to let British Transport Police know that we no longer require their surveillance."

"Ma'am," Lottie nodded and went back to the incident room.

41

EDINBURGH AIRPORT

N ow that his plan had been set in motion and he'd gone through the airport security check point, Anthony Kelly breathed a sigh of relief and he felt calmer and more composed. The events of the past hour and a half had unnerved him but he smiled to himself now, imagining himself like any other holiday maker passing the time until his flight was called.

He wandered around the shops in the 'after security' area of the terminal which was accessible only to those with tickets and who had gone through the security scanners.

He was amazed at the number and assortment of shops. It was almost like walking along Princes Street, he thought, with the usual well known names selling everything from sports gear to duty free alcohol. There was even one called, 'The Sunglass Hut' and he stood gazing, wide eyed, at the window display, unable to believe the range and the price of the items: Ray Ban £200; Versace: £250; Prada £350. "They're having a laugh" he thought to himself and yet, inside the shop, people were trying them on and buying them from persuasive shop assistants.

Just at that moment there was an announcement and a disembodied voice said: "First call for passengers on flight EZY302 to Gatwick, please proceed to Gate 3. Passengers on flight EZY302 to Gatwick, please proceed to gate 3."

Kelly looked around him, a little disoriented. He had wandered far into the shopping mall and had to get his bearings again. Then he saw signs directing passengers to the various departure gates and he followed the signs for Gate 3 for what seemed a long way, until he saw a small seated waiting area where his flight number was displayed under 'Gate 3 Departure Lounge'.

He sat down with the other passengers who were waiting to board the Gatwick flight. He was now eager to get on the plane and leave Edinburgh and this morning's nightmare behind. He felt as though he had been in the airport for hours and hours and yet, when he looked at his watch, he saw that it had been less than two hours.

42

A LITTLE TIME LATER

While Kelly sat waiting to board his flight to freedom, as he thought of it now, he was blissfully unaware of all the frantic coordinated activity of Northumbria Police and Police Scotland.

Six officers had been dispatched to the airport and cautioned to adopt a 'softly, softly' approach to Kelly, who had already killed one man in cold blood. They had been instructed to keep him under observation and to wait until all the passengers were on board the plane. The airline boarding crew had been informed of the situation and would give the police the signal that they would lead him to where Kelly was seated on the plane.

The announcement to board the flight was made. "Passengers on flight EZY302 to Gatwick is now boarding. Please make your way to the desk and have your boarding pass ready for inspection," the voice announced from the ether.

Kelly joined the queue of passengers waiting to have their passes checked and be directed to their seats on the plane.

When he got to the front of the queue, the smiling flight

attendant greeted him, checked his boarding pass and directed him down the aisle to seat 21C, then she nodded to the police officers who were waiting out of sight of the remaining passengers waiting to board.

Their instructions were to wait until the last passenger had boarded and then the flight attendant would lead them to where Kelly was seated.

KELLY PUT his holdall in the overhead compartment and settled into his seat. There was only one other person in the row of three and she was in the window seat. He was pleased that there was an empty seat between them as he hated being squashed up against other people. Since having a severe bout of Covid the previous year, he was wary of catching viruses of any kind. He took the small bottle of antibacterial gel, that he always carried in his pocket, and squeezed a liberal amount into the palm of his hand before thoroughly massaging it into his hands and between his fingers. Only when this was done would he fasten his safety belt.

All this time, the jet's engines had been turning noisily, keeping the cabin air conditioned and then they stopped suddenly. The silence now, after the constant whine was deafening.

Kelly was aware of someone standing next to his aisle seat and thought it was just the flight attendant making sure everyone's safety belt was fastened for take off. However, when the figure didn't move on, he looked up to see two uniformed police officers standing in the aisle. Fear shot through him, like a thousand shards of glass, and he knew there was no escape.

"Mr Anthony Kelly?" the police officer said, "I would like you to come with us Sir."

He looked wildly down the aisle, towards the cockpit, and then back to the open door, which he'd so naively thought was his escape route from anyone pursuing him and he realised he was trapped. He stood up and one officer handcuffed him and led him back along the aisle to the door, while the other followed behind.

Once off the plane, the officers stopped and one of them said "Anthony Kelly I am arresting you on suspicion of the murder of Fr Michael Donovan at his home on Holy Island on Friday the 15th September." He was then read his rights and led away.

Outside the terminal building they took Kelly to where three police cars waited with their lights flashing. "Mind your head Sir," an officer said as they put him into the first car.

People going in and out of the terminal building stood watching and speculated amongst themselves, some wondering whether he was a terrorist and worrying that their flight would be delayed, or even cancelled.

"Where are you taking me?" he asked, once he was in the car, "and where's my luggage?"

"Your belongings have been retrieved from the plane Sir and we have instructions to take you to Berwick Police Station where you will be in the custody of Northumbria Police and questioned by the murder investigation team there."

They drove off towards the Edinburgh City Bypass on their way south, down the A1. One of the waiting cars went ahead as an escort, lights flashing to expedite their journey to Berwick-upon-Tweed.

43

BERWICK POLICE STATION

I t was eleven forty-five when Anthony Kelly and his police escort arrived at Berwick Police Station and they handed their suspect over to the Custody Sergeant for processing.

During the following thirty minutes, Kelly had his finger prints and a DNA sample taken and was photographed front and profile.

"Do you understand why you've been arrested?" the Custody Sergeant asked him.

"Somethin' to do wi' the murder o' some priest," replied a surly Kelly and he added belligerently, "Ah don't know any priest and Ah want a lawyer."

"We'll come to that in a minute Sir," and the sergeant added by way of explanation, "I'm authorising your detention so that you can be interviewed regarding information the police have received and this will give you the opportunity to give your side of the story, okay?"

"Ah suppose so. Ah don't have much choice in the matter though, do Ah?" Kelly replied.

"Would you like a solicitor Mr Kelly?" the sergeant asked.

"Aye, Ah would but Ah don't have one as such."

"That's alright Sir, a solicitor will be appointed for you."

The sergeant turned to the Custody Assistant and said, "Take Mr Kelly to cell M1 please."

Kelly screwed his nose up as he entered the area of holding cells and asked, "What the hell is that awful smell?"

It was a mixture of bleach and disinfectant, with strong overtones of urine and faeces.

"That's just the usual Custody Suite aroma mate," replied his escort, "You'll get used to it if you're here long enough."

Kelly walked into the cell and the door slammed shut with a disconcerting finality. He sat in the small tiled room and put his head in his hands, wondering how on earth he was going to get himself out of this desperate mess.

"Ah only hope the lawyer they gie' me is a good one an' no' one that looks like they've just left school," he said to the empty room, "Ma only chance is tae have a modern day equivalent o' Joseph Beltrami.

44

INCIDENT ROOM

MONDAY AFTERNOON

DCI Flynn had been informed of the arrest and detention of Anthony Kelly and, as Senior Investigating Officer, he had travelled to Berwick.

His role was to liaise with the Crown Prosecution Service and to assess and approve the interview strategy which was in the process of being drawn up by DS Lockhart and DC Dean for the formal questioning of the prisoner which was scheduled for that afternoon.

The 'clock was ticking' on the length of time that prisoners could be held in custody, so time was also a factor, and Flynn had informed them of his intention to observe at least some of the interview via a video link in the station.

A duty solicitor had been appointed for Kelly and he was travelling up from Morpeth that afternoon, so Kelly would get the opportunity to discuss the reason for his arrest before the interview took place

Since the time of Kelly's arrest at Edinburgh Airport, DC Dean, who was a trained interviewer with years of experience interviewing the suspects of serious crimes, had been preparing an interview strategy to elicit the information they would need in order to charge Kelly with the priest's murder.

The fingerprints taken from Kelly were found to be a match for those lifted by forensics at the murder scene, although it would be forty-eight to seventy-two hours before the result of the DNA sample would be back.

Dean had finalised the interview strategy at two-thirty and he took it to DI Clelland who wanted to look at it before its final scrutiny by the Senior Investigating Officer.

They had Kelly in detention for twenty-four hours and any further detention, if it was deemed necessary, would have to be agreed by the superintendent. Dean was quietly confident that they would be able to charge Kelly within the initial detention period.

45

THE INTERVIEW
MONDAY 1500 HOURS

The interview room in Berwick police Station was a windowless, rather airless space with grey walls and a table that was screwed into the floor.

Since his arrival at Berwick just before midday, Anthony Kelly had been fed and watered. A plastic cup of water had been set on the table where the suspect would be placed.

At two-forty Kelly was taken from his cell to the interview room where he had an in-depth conversation with his defence solicitor, Mr William Prendergast, of Prendergast, Brown and Manson, which was a prestigious law firm with offices in Newcastle and Morpeth.

Kelly had felt relieved when he saw that Prendergast was a man in his fifties and, in fact, was a senior partner in the law firm. Kelly, rightly or wrongly, believed an experienced older solicitor would serve him better than a younger, less experienced man or woman.

At five minutes to three, Dean was informed that both client and legal representative were ready for the interview and he and Lottie, who was to sit in, went downstairs. Clelland and Flynn went into another room to observe the interview via the video link that had been set up for them.

Kelly was cautioned and Dean pressed the video record button.

"Interview commenced at 15.02. Present are DC Gary Dean, DS Lottie Lockhart." He looked across the table at Kelly and said, "Please state your name for the record."

"Anthony Gerard Kelly."

"William Prendargast, defence solicitor."

Dean opened the interview by saying, "Mr Kelly, we are investigating the murder of Fr Michael Donovan in his home on the Holy Island of Lindisfarne on the night of Friday the fifteenth of September." Dean was looking directly at Kelly who allowed only brief eye contact before averting his gaze.

"Can you tell me how you came to know Fr Donovan?"

"Ah never said Ah knew him," replied Kelly.

"Are you saying that you did not know the deceased Mr Kelly?"

"Aye, Ah'm sayin' that Ah didnae ken the priest fae Adam." Kelly stared defiantly at Dean but his leg was shaking uncontrollably below the table.

"Okay then, can you tell me where you were during the hours of 9am on Friday the fifteenth of September and 2am on Saturday the sixteenth?"

"Well, Ah'd be workin' on the Friday an' then Ah was at home all night. Ah watched TV and had a few cans, wi' it bein' the weekend like."

"Where do you work?"

"Ah work for the roads department o' Edinburgh City Council," he replied confidently, comfortable with the question.

"Do you own a car Mr Kelly?"

"No, Ah cannae afford a car on ma wages."

"Do you have a driving licence? Can you drive a car?"

"Aye, of course Ah can drive, Ah needed tae have a drivin' licence for ma work."

"Have you ever been to Holy Island Mr Kelly?" Dean asked.

"Ah cannae remember," Kelly replied.

"You can't remember visiting a place that people come from all over to see? I mean, even the name of the place makes it sound special - Holy Island - and you don't remember if you've been there?" Dean asked, sounding puzzled but non confrontational.

"Ah might have been taken by ma folks when Ah was a bairn, but if Ah was, Ah don't remember it," Kelly replied, shifting in his seat and beginning to look wary.

Mr Prendergast interrupted, "Are my client's childhood outings relevant Detective Constable?"

"Very" was Dean's terse reply.

Kelly looked at his solicitor who nodded, almost imperceptibly, for him to continue to answer the questions.

"Where did you go to school Mr Kelly?" Dean then asked.

"Eh? ... What?" Kelly stammered, surprised at this change in the direction of the questions.

"Which primary school did you attend Mr Kelly?" Dean rephrased the question.

"St David's Primary School in Edinburgh," Kelly replied.

Prendergast stopped writing in his leather bound notepad and glared at Dean but resisted interrupting. Dean ignored him and continued with his questions.

"You said you were at home on the Friday evening having 'a few cans' and watching TV. Was anyone with you?

Can anybody confirm that you were at home watching the television?"

"Naw, Ah was on ma own," Kelly replied gruffly, "Ah'm 'Tony Nae Mates'," he added self-mockingly.

"Can you remember what programmes you were watching?" Dean then asked.

There was a slight pause before Kelly responded and, with a smile he said, "The news channel. Ah was watchin' the news channel," he nodded, thinking he had put one over on the detective and added, "Ah like tae keep up wi' current affairs." He folded his big muscular arms across his chest.

"And what were those current affairs that were being reported on, on the night of Friday the fifteenth of September, Mr Kelly?" Dean probed.

Kelly was momentarily stunned, then recovering, he waved a meaty hand and said, "Och, you know, politics, inflation, climate change," he shrugged his shoulders.

"Was there anything specific that stood out that night Mr Kelly?"

"No really, it just a' blends thegither, especially after a few cans. Ah probably fell asleep," he paused, then added, "Aye, that's right, Ah did fa' asleep and Ah woke up around one o'clock in the mornin', maybe half past one, so Ah switched off the telly an' went tae ma kip."

"And you have no one who can corroborate that?" asked Dean.

"Nae such luck pal!" he laughed suggestively.

Neither detective acknowledged this remark and Dean continued. "Let me take you back to Friday the fifteenth of September. You told us that you were at work that day Mr Kelly, is that correct?"

Mr Prendergast interrupted again. "Detective Constable Dean my client has already answered that question," then looking at the expensive watch on his wrist, he added, "now can we get on? I'm a busy man."

Dean ignored the interruption and looked at Kelly. He scratched his head and made a point of looking at the file in front of him.

"You see Mr Kelly, I have a bit of a problem with that. Your employer has told us that you were not at work that day, that you had, in fact, taken a day's annual leave on Friday the fifteenth of September."

Both client and solicitor looked at each other before Kelly said, "They're mistaken, Ah was definitely at work that day. Ask any o' ma work mates, we were resurfacing the High Street just ootside St Gile's Cathedral."

"So your work got that wrong, did they?"

"They did, ask ma work mates." Kelly repeated.

"You told us that you did not know the murder victim, Fr Michael Donovan. You said that you 'didn't know him from Adam'. Are you sure about that?" Dean asked, watching Kelly carefully.

"Aye," Kelly replied, but he was becoming less confident under the detective's steady gaze and questioning. His foot was now beating a tattoo on the floor and the solicitor was looking at his client quizzically.

"Detective," Prendergast interrupted yet again but Dean waved the interruption away, saying, "Let me get this clear Mr Kelly, you're saying that you didn't know Fr Donovan and yet he was the chaplain to St David's Primary School for a long number of years, including," he referred to his file again, "when you attended the primary school."

Mr Prendergast whispered something to Kelly and Dean went on.

"Your finger prints were found in Fr Donovan's cottage

the day after he was killed. How do you account for that Mr Kelly?"

Kelly stared at his hands in his lap and said, "No comment."

"I'll ask you again Mr Kelly, how did your fingerprints come to be in Fr Donovan's cottage?"

"No comment."

"Okay, your finger prints were found on the doorbell of the priest's cottage and on a bottle of whisky and a glass in the sitting room of the cottage. Can you tell me how your finger prints came to be there Mr Kelly?" Dean tried asking the question another way.

"No comment."

"What happened to your brother Michael?"

Kelly's head shot up as though Dean had struck him, then he quickly looked down again and said, "No comment."

"We have received information that your brother, Michael, had been one of the many boys known to have been sexually abused by Fr Donovan when they were members of the church choir. We also know that on the fifteenth of September 2013 your brother took his own life by hanging himself in his bedroom in your parents' home, having suffered from mental illness for a number of years."

Dean paused and let the information sink in for a few moments, then added, "Now I would say that is a pretty strong motive for murder."

"No comment."

"Shall I tell you what I think happened Mr Kelly?"

There was no response, not even a 'no comment'.

"I think you went to the priest's house on the tenth anniversary of your brother's death to kill the man you held responsible for all the years that Michael had suffered from a mental illness and for his subsequent suicide."

"No comment."

"And that's why your finger prints came to be at the murder scene and why a witness saw you in the vicinity at the time in question," Dean pushed his point.

"No comment."

"In addition to your finger prints, we also have other evidence that places you at the murder scene."

Before his client could repeat his 'no comment' response, Prendergast said, "I would like to have a conference with my client please, Detective Constable Dean."

Dean nodded and said, "Interview suspended at 15.47." He stopped the recording and both he and Lottie left the room.

Flynn was in the incident room when Gary and Lottie returned. Lottie put the kettle on to make a cup of tea for them both.

Flynn said, "Good work Dean, you've got him on the ropes, I think we can have this wrapped up today."

"Sir," Gary replied, gratefully accepting the tea that Lottie handed him.

"Would you like a chocolate digestive to go with that Gary?" Lottie asked, rummaging through her capacious bag.

"Aye, why not? I'm a bit peckish," he replied smiling.

During the break, Kelly's solicitor had been advised of the CCTV footage, clearly placing his client near the priest's cottage.

46

THE INTERVIEW CONTINUES

1700 HOURS

The interview of Anthony Kelly resumed at five o'clock. Dean pressed the record button and said, "Interview resumes at 17.00 hours. Mr Kelly, Mr Prendergast, Detective Sergeant Lockhart and Detective Constable Gary Dean are present."

Mr Prendergast spoke, "I thank you for giving me the time to confer with my client and, on his behalf, I will read out the following statement:

"I admit that I did know Fr Donovan and I did go to visit him on the anniversary of my twin brother Michael's death, but I swear I did not kill him. I went to see him on Friday afternoon because I wanted to have it out with him. I admit that I was angry about Michael committing suicide and I wanted Fr Donovan to know that I blamed him for Michael's mental health problems over the years. Fr Donovan cried and told me he was sorry and I left it at that. Fr Donovan was alive and well when I left his cottage."

"Thank you Mr Prendergast," said Dean, "Mr Kelly will be returned to his cell now. In the meantime, we will consult with the Crown Prosecution Service regarding charges against your client." He stopped the recording.

As Senior Investigating Officer, DCI Flynn had been keeping the CPS informed as the case progressed and, having considered all the evidence, along with the suspect's statement, the Crown Prosecution Service made the decision to charge Anthony Kelly with the murder of Fr Michael Donovan.

At six-twenty they found themselves back in the interview room once again. Dean switched on the video recorder and said, "Interview resumes at 18.20. Mr Kelly, Mr Prendergast. Detective Sergeant Lockhart and Detective Constable Dean are present."

There was a short silence, then Dean said, "Anthony Kelly you are charged with the following offence. You do not have to say anything unless you wish to do so but it may harm your defence if you do not mention now something that you later rely on in court. Anything you do say may be used in evidence. That you, Anthony Gerard Kelly on the fifteenth of September murdered Michael Donovan, contrary to common law. Interview terminated at 18.25."

"Ah didnae dae it! Ah never killed him," Kelly protested loudly and repeatedly, as he was led back to his cell.

47

MONDAY EVENING
EDINBURGH

I n her little ground floor flat at 100 Slateford Road Edinburgh, Elsie McLaren switched off her television.

Tears were running freely down her wrinkled old face and she felt as though she had suffered a terrible bereavement. Her lovely laddie, as she thought of him, had been arrested and charged with the murder of the priest on Holy Island and he would probably go to gaol for a very long time.

She had just watched the ten o'clock news where she heard Detective Chief Inspector Flynn, of Northumbria Police, make a statement to the media where he had thanked the public for their help in apprehending the man accused of the murder of the Catholic priest on Holy Island ten days before.

In his atement he had paid tribute to Police Scotland for their cooperation in bringing Kelly into police custody.

Mrs McLaren sat in her quiet living room and wondered what she would do without Tony's visits and the help he gave her.

"Whae's gonnae go for ma messages now Tony?" she

asked the empty room. "Maybe the polis got it wrong and it wisnae Tony that killed the auld priest" she said. "Ah jist cannae believe that a laddie that went oot o' his way tae help an auld wummin like me could have done such a thing."

She had been fretting ever since the two police officers had entered the building that morning, looking for Tony. "Fancy breakin' doon yer door like that son!" she said, as though he was there, sitting in her living room and having a cup of tea with her. "An' Ah kept watchin' for you gettin' off the number 35 bus after work, but ye never did."

Fresh tears flowed and she was worried that without Tony's help, Jenny, her great niece and only living relative, would push for her to go into a care home. She'd been trying for the past year and a half to get her Auntie Elsie to go into a home, claiming she wasn't fit to look after herself but, with Tony's help, she'd managed to resist her attempts to relieve herself of the burden of the old auntie whom she hardly ever visited.

"What have Ah got left now?" she asked, "Ah've naebody an' ma memory an ma arthritis is gettin' so bad that Ah really relied on Tony droppin' in after work an' makin' sure Ah wis a'right."

She breathed a sigh that seemed to come from the soles of her feet, the exhalation fluttered unevenly, as it left her aged lungs. She sat back in her chair and closed her eyes for the last time, her grief over Tony had been too much for her aching heart to bear.

48

TUESDAY 26TH SEPTEMBER
BERWICK MAGISTRATES COURT

Anthony Kelly appeared before the Magistrates Court the following morning where he made a plea of 'not guilty'.

He was remanded in custody, as requested by the Crown Prosecution Service, to await trial by jury in a Crown Court at some future date. Both Detective Sergeant Lottie Lockhart and Detective Constable Gary Dean were present in court to witness the preliminary hearing.

When they emerged into the autumn sunshine, Lottie breathed in the fresh air and sighed with relief and satisfaction.

"Thank goodness that's over," said Gary.

"Well, not quite Gary," Lottie replied, "there is still the substantial matter of all the paperwork to complete as well as any loose ends, but I know what you mean."

"Come on, I'll treat you to a cafe latte," Gary offered.

"Can you afford it Gary? Let me buy it." Lottie said.

"Nah! My finances can run to a decent coffee since it's a special occasion. It'll kick start us on all that paperwork you were talking about."

"Okay, if you're sure, " she said, "but before I start on that I need to check in with the station sergeant and see what's happening with my stalker of an ex husband."

"Okay, I'll grab the coffees and see you upstairs."

49

HONEY BEE COTTAGE
THAT EVENING

When Lottie let herself into the cottage after work, Frank was already there and the delicious aroma of cooking filled the house. Dolly was, literally, on top of her before she could get the door shut.

"Hello Dolly Dimples," she said patting the ecstatic hound, "Mam's early tonight, isn't she and you're so happy to see me back early for a change, aren't you?" Dolly's tail was windmilling as Lottie fussed over her.

After a few minutes of patting her, Dolly had calmed down and she said, "Good girl! Now go and sit on the sofa while I give Frank a kiss."

When she entered the kitchen, Frank was opening a bottle of champagne. He poured the sparkling, pale liquid into crystal champagne flutes and handed one to Lottie.

"Here's to the successful outcome of your investigation Pet," he said and he clinked his glass against hers.

"Thank you Frank." She sipped the champagne and coughed a little as the bubbles caught her breath. "What's cooking love? It smells divine."

"Stir-fry and noodles," he replied.

"Now I could get used to this," she said appreciatively, sipping her drink and looking tenderly at Frank.

LATER THAT NIGHT, as they sat cuddled up on the sofa in front of the fire, Lottie turned to Frank and kissed him on the lips. "Thank you Frank, for being such a support these past days, I don't know how I would have managed without you."

"Aw, ye're welcome Pet. Ah'm just glad Ah was able to help you out."

Earlier, during supper, she had told him about the injunction that had been made against Denis McIvor. He was banned from coming within a fifty mile radius of Honey Bee Cottage and Lottie, any breach of which would be regarded as a violation of his release conditions and he could end up back in prison.

With that and the CCTV doorbells that had been installed that morning, she felt she could now relax and feel safe again in her own home.

She sighed contentedly and took Frank's hand as they sat in the softly lit room. She turned to him and said, "I do love you Frank and I meant it earlier, when I said I could get used to this."

He looked at her, not daring to believe that she was saying what he hoped she was saying. Then with the question in his eyes, he said, "You mean ...?"

She squeezed his hand and nodded, saying, "When do you want to move in Frank love?"

50

MORPETH

FRIDAY 29TH SEPTEMBER

D etectives Lockhart and Dean had spent a few days finishing off the paperwork after Kelly had been charged and remanded in custody. Then they took the opportunity to have some well earned annual leave.

Now that the stress of the investigation was over Gary thought he should be feeling better than he actually was. However, the truth was that he had time to dwell on the depressing circumstances of his life.

After rallying from thoughts of suicide the previous weekend, he was once again plunged into a dark place. He wouldn't be able to see his solicitor, to begin the proceedings to sell the family home, for another week and thoughts of the childhood abuse triggered by the murder of Fr Donovan, still plagued him.

It was almost midday by the time he managed to drag himself out of bed and into the shower. He stood under the slow-flowing tepid water and wondered what he could do to pull himself out of this stultifying mood.

As he rinsed the last of the shampoo from his hair he

remembered the conversation he'd had with Lottie on the way back from interviewing Philip Hughes in Edinburgh. She was such a good listener and he decided he would call her after he'd had some tea and toast, perhaps he could meet up with her for a chat.

Half an hour later he speed dialled her number, a little apprehensive at the thought of asking her for a favour.

"Hello Gary," she said cheerily when she answered his call, "how are you enjoying your first day off in ages?"

"Well, that's the thing Lottie and I'm sorry to bother you," he began, "but I was wondering if I could maybe talk to you about ... you know ..." he was struggling to find the words, "well, what we talked about in the car coming back from Edinburgh like," he finished lamely.

"Of course, it's no bother. Do you want to come here?" she replied.

"Well if that's alright with you, but I thought Frank was staying with you for a few days?" He sounded unsure. "I wouldn't want to spoil your plans like."

"No, that's okay," she said, sounding happier now the investigation into the priest's murder was solved. "Frank is moving in with us and he's going back to Newcastle to get some things and organise his flat, so he'll be away all afternoon," she explained. "When should I expect you?"

"I'll leave soon so I should be with you about," he looked at his watch, "half past two, quarter to three."

"Perfect," she replied. "We're just going to have some lunch and then Frank will set off. He won't be back here until this evening so we'll have plenty of time to talk Gary."

"Thanks, you're a life saver Lottie. See you soon!" he said and hung up.

51

HONEY BEE COTTAGE

THAT AFTERNOON

Lottie kissed Frank goodbye at the door of the cottage. "Drive safely Frank and we'll see you this evening. Text me when you're on your way home and I'll make a start on supper."

"Will do, have a great chat with Gary. Give him my regards," he said, then going to the sitting room window he blew Dolly a kiss and waved. Dolly was in the habit of standing up on her hind legs with her front paws on the window sill when Frank left the cottage, so she could watch him until he got into the car and drove away.

"Bye Dolly Girl! Bye Lottie, see you later!"

Lottie went inside and washed up the lunch dishes, singing happily to herself. It felt good to have the investigation successfully behind the team and she was enjoying the freedom of having time off when she didn't have to think about anything other than relaxing for the next few days.

As she put the last of the dishes back in the cupboard Jane appeared at the kitchen door and Lottie beckoned to her to come in.

"It is such a beautiful day Lottie and I was wondering if you and Dolly would like to come for a walk with me," she said. "I thought a long walk along the other side of the river on the Ladykirk estate would be grand on a day like today. Are you up for it?"

"That sounds lovely Jane, but I'm expecting a visitor soon. It's a shame since it's such a good day for a long walk along the Tweed."

"Ah, not to worry Lottie," Jane replied, "I'll go anyway. Why don't I take Dolly with me?"

On hearing Jane's voice Dolly had come into the kitchen, tail wagging in greeting at one of her favourite people. Jane stroked her head and asked, "Would you like to go walkies with Auntie Jane?"

Dolly's tail windmilled in response and Lottie said, "I think that is a 'yes' Jane."

Lottie clipped Dolly's lead onto her collar and said, "Actually Jane, my visitor is coming for a heart-to-heart talk, so would you mind keeping Dolly for a couple of hours or so? I wouldn't want her bursting in at a delicate moment, if you know what I mean."

"Of course, I don't mind. She can stay with me until your visitor has gone, just come and get her when you're ready."

"Thank you Jane." Lottie rubbed Dolly's ears and said, "Now you be a good girl for Jane, Dolly Dimples, and I'll see you later."

THE DOORBELL RANG at two-thirty and Lottie went to the door to let Gary in. The welcoming smile on her face turned to horror as she was pushed back against the wall. A rough hand covered her mouth before she could utter a cry for help.

It was her ex husband, Denis McIvor. He kicked the front door shut on any help that might have been on the street outside.

"You didn't think a fucking piece of paper was going to keep me away, did you Lottie?" His voice was low and menacing and his lip curled as he said, "Are you scared? You should be."

She felt her blood run cold as waves of fear ran through her, echoes of past threats returning.

Keeping one hand over her mouth, he grabbed her right arm and pulled it behind her back, holding her wrist in a vice-like grip, her shoulder felt like it was about to dislocate.

Denis McIvor was over six feet tall and well built and he propelled her along the hallway. Lottie tried to bite the huge hand over her mouth and failed to penetrate the thick fingers. Then with her free hand she struggled to pull his hand away but he tightened the grip on her mouth so firmly that she felt her teeth cut into the soft fleshy inside of her mouth.

"Aren't you going to give me a tour of your cosy home Lottie dear? I wonder where the bedroom might be?" he hissed into her ear as he pushed her in front of him. The thought of him in her bedroom made her feel nauseous with a combination of disgust and fear.

The terror of years ago came back in a rush and she felt a panic that seemed to rob her of the ability to breathe. She was convinced she would die of fright even before he did another thing to her.

He found the bedroom at the back of the cottage and pushed her roughly onto the bed. He released the hand on her mouth to reach into his jacket pocket for something and she screamed as loud as she could, hoping to attract the attention of a neighbour who might happen to be in their back garden, but he quickly clamped his hand over her mouth again, stifling her screams.

He got onto the bed and knelt astride her, pinning her arms by her sides with his knees. It was duct tape that he'd taken out of his pocket and he pulled off a strip to cover her mouth.

When she realised what his intention was she thrashed her head from side to side but the sticky material caught her hair painfully and suddenly her mouth and nose were covered with the vile stuff.

She was unable to breathe and she panicked as she suffocated. Just as she was about to pass out he uncovered the tape from her nose and she inhaled noisily, trying to take in as much air as possible through her nostrils.

He had an evil glint in his eyes as he said, "You didn't think I was going to let you suffocate, did you Lottie dear?"

The threatening undercurrent was palpable. She tried to scream but the only sound to emerge was a weak whimper. She attempted once more to wrest her arms free but he had her arms pinned to her side by his knees and her legs were immobile under his weight.

"No my dear Lottie, of course not. I wouldn't let you suffocate," he said, sheer malice dripping from his words. "I want you to be conscious. I want you to be fully aware and know what's happening to you as we share these last precious moments together."

He shrugged out of his jacket and she could see, from the T-shirt that was straining over the bulging arms and chest muscles, that during his time inside, he had made good use of the prison gym.

Her eyes were wide with terror, not knowing what he was going to do next. She could see that he was enjoying this power of life and death that he was holding over her. She tried to calm her breathing and not give in to the fear.

She needed to think rationally, but this was even worse than her nightmares, she knew this was no bad dream and she wasn't going to suddenly wake up from it.

All she could think of was that she was so glad Jane had taken Dolly since she knew this evil bastard would have taken great pleasure from hurting and killing her beloved pet in front of her eyes.

He was speaking again, his face only an inch from hers, as he held her head still so she couldn't look away. She shut her eyes on the cruelty that was clearly etched on his face and felt she was losing the battle to be calm.

Her eyes were forced open when she felt his hands around her throat and he said, "You haven't forgotten what I told you, have you Lottie? Remember I told you that you could run but you couldn't hide ... and here we are." She hated hearing him say her name. It besmirched it somehow, coming from him.

"I always keep my promises and when you left for work that day ... and never came home ..." he feigned sadness, "I promised myself that I would track you down and pay you back."

He loosened his belt buckle and unzipped his trousers with one hand while keeping hold of her throat with the other.

Her terror deepened and she began to feel as though she was floating up towards the ceiling, a calmness suffusing through her until she was above herself, looking down on what was happening in the room below.

The sudden shrill ringing of the doorbell caused McIvor

to loosen his hold on her neck and she felt herself back on the bed once more, with a dull thud.

"Gary!" she thought, lucid again, "I'd totally forgotten about Gary. What will he do when I don't answer the door?"

GARY STOOD outside the front door, puzzled that Lottie didn't answer it. He looked at his watch and it was now three o'clock. He had been held up on the A1 due to an accident and the traffic had been diverted off the main road and through little Northumberland villages before rejoining the A1 again near Haggerston.

He rang the bell again and banged on the door but Lottie still wasn't answering it. He looked through the sitting room window but there was no sign of Lottie or Dolly, either there or in the kitchen beyond. He wondered if she was in the back garden talking to a neighbour and she hadn't heard the doorbell, so he walked around the side of the cottage to the back, but there was no one to be seen.

He peered through the bedroom window, shading his eyes so he could see in and he was shocked to see a man kneeling over a figure lying on the bed. He knew it was Lottie on the bed and that she was in grave danger.

The man had his back to the window and was unaware of Gary's presence, although he must have heard the door-bell. Thoughts sped through Gary's mind as he frantically tried to decide what to do next.

He hurried to the back door and was relieved to find it was unlocked. He quietly let himself into the kitchen and was looking around for a suitable weapon when his eyes fell on a heavy cast-iron frying pan hanging from a hook on the wall.

He crept silently through the cottage and stopped at the door of Lottie's bedroom and listened, assessing the situation. He heard muffled frightened, almost animal-like sounds coming from the room. It was Lottie, trying to scream for help.

Taking a deep breath, Gary burst into the room and, as McIvor began to turn his head, he hit him as hard as he could with the heavy pan. With a grunt, McIvor slumped, unconscious, on top of Lottie.

WHEN THE DOOR bell had stopped ringing, Denis McIvor thought whoever it was had got fed up and gone away. He was breathing raggedly, in an aroused state and intent solely on raping his ex wife, before slowly killing her. He had taken his hand from her throat, had roughly pulled her skirt up and began ripping her underwear off when he felt a sudden crack on the back of his head.

It took Gary only a few moments to haul the prone body of McIvor off and away from Lottie, who struggled to sit up. She painfully peeled the tape from her face and hair before gulping in air, like a drowning person rescued from water.

"Oh Gary!" she cried still struggling to breathe, "Oh Gary, he was going to kill me!"

At that moment McIvor groaned and Lottie pointed and said, "Quick, get the duct tape!"

Gary caught on immediately and roughly hauled McIvor's hands behind his back then taped them tightly together before doing the same with his ankles.

He took Lottie's hand and helped her off the bed. "Are you alright Lottie? Can you stand up?" She nodded, holding on to Gary's arm for support.

They stood by the bedroom door and Gary took his phone from his pocket and called 999. He asked for police and an ambulance, quickly explaining who he was and that there had been an attempted rape and murder.

McIvor was still semi conscious and groaning when Gary said, "Come into the sitting room Lottie, he's not going anywhere in a hurry."

Lottie gratefully allowed herself to be led away from her bedroom where her ex husband had been terrorising her, almost beyond her endurance.

She was shaking uncontrollably now and Gary put her in her chair by the fire. He went to the kitchen and brought back a glass of water and held it to her lips as her trembling hands couldn't hold it.

She took a few sips, breathed in deeply and said, "Brandy," pointing to the corner cupboard where glasses and bottles of spirits were kept.

"Here, sip this slowly," Gary said when he'd brought her the drink, then they heard the approaching sirens of police and ambulance vehicles as they drew up outside Honey Bee Cottage.

THE PARAMEDICS GAVE McIvor a quick check-up and confirmed he was fit enough to be arrested, knowing that the police medical officer would examine him at the station. He was cautioned and taken away by two of the police officers while the other two remained behind to take statements from Lottie and Gary.

Lottie refused to go to hospital but agreed to the female paramedic checking her over. Her throat ached painfully where it had been cruelly squeezed by McIvor's big hands but she was otherwise alright, though very badly shaken and in a state of shock.

After the police and paramedics had gone Lottie said in a barely audible croak, "Thank God you arrived when you did Gary, he was going to ... he was going to ..." She couldn't bring herself to say the words "rape me".

"It's alright Lottie," he soothed, "you don't have to say it, I know what you mean."

She smiled her gratitude and he continued, "I would have been here sooner but there was a crash on the A1 near Belford and the traffic was diverted."

"He must have been watching and saw Frank leave before coming to the door. I thought it was you and I opened it without even checking the CCTV." She shook her head, "How could I have been so stupid? I should have known a court order wouldn't be a barrier to *him*."

"Don't be so hard on yourself Lottie," Gary said, "The blame lies entirely with him, not you. You know that deep down."

"I know you're right Gary," she said, adding, "I'm just so relieved that Jane had taken Dolly for the afternoon, the alternative doesn't bear thinking about. That evil bastard would have beaten Dolly just for the pleasure of causing me pain."

As though saying her name had conjured her up, Dolly came trotting into the room, followed by an anxious Jane.

"I saw the ambulance and police car leave as we came along West Street. What on earth has happened? Are you alright Lottie?"

While Lottie stroked Dolly, who was aware that something was amiss, she told Jane about her terrifying experience, including the earlier stalking and the subsequent injunction.

"Well I hope they throw away the key this time!" Jane said, "You've had a very lucky escape, thanks to this young man," she said, patting Gary on the shoulder. "Well, if you're sure you're alright, I'll leave you in peace."

"I'm fine," Lottie said hoarsely and Jane hugged her friend and went home.

"Do you want me to stay with you until Frank arrives, Lottie?" Gary asked after Jane had gone.

"Oh Gary, I'm sorry, you wanted to have a talk with me," Lottie replied.

"Aw, it's okay Lottie. To be honest, it doesn't seem that important now, although it will probably creep up on me again at some point."

"Let me know if and when you want to talk about it Gary."

Lottie began to tremble again, as the horror of what Gary had saved her from hit her once more. Gary took a crocheted throw from the back of the sofa and wrapped it around her shoulders.

"I'll make you some sweet tea and I'll wait with you until Frank gets back. I don't want to leave you on your own when you're still in shock."

The tea seemed to rally Lottie and she and Gary managed to have the talk scheduled for earlier that afternoon. By the time Frank arrived home Lottie was much calmer and Gary left, knowing that Lottie needed to tell Frank what had happened on her own.

After a long talk and much cosseting by Frank, Lottie was more or less back to her old self after a few hours.

The police charges against McIvor would have been set in motion by now and she felt safer knowing he was behind bars and would be for a long time to come. It was not guaranteed, but more than likely that he would not be considered for parole at the end of his second term in prison.

Dolly was lying in her usual place in front of the fire, snoring gently, and Lottie was enveloped in Frank's arms. She smiled and sighed, all was well in their world once again.

FIVE MONTHS LATER

EPILOGUE

On Friday the sixteenth of February, the Evening Chronicle reported on the trial of Anthony Kelly.

"PRIEST KILLER CONVICTED

The trial of Anthony Kelly, who was accused of the murder of Fr Michael Donovan in his home on Holy Island last September, has been heard over the past two weeks in the Crown Court here at The Quays in Newcastle.

The jury, comprising of seven women and five men had retired for a matter of just three hours and forty minutes to consider their verdict. When they returned to the court room, the fore person was asked if they'd reached a verdict.

"Yes." She replied.

"Do you find the defendant guilty or not guilty?" asked the Clerk of the Court.

"Guilty." she said solemnly.

"Is that the verdict of you all?"

"It is," she confirmed.

The Judge, Mrs Justice Hemmings, addressed the prisoner in the dock.

"You have been found guilty of the murder of Michael Donovan by a unanimous verdict.

Anthony Gerard Kelly, I sentence you to life imprisonment, with a minimum term of twenty-five years. The term reflects the premeditated nature of your crime and the fact that you persistently made pleas of 'not guilty', thereby incurring much time and expense on the part of the court. Case dismissed."

She banged the gavel and the court rose as the prisoner was led away, head bowed, to begin his life sentence in a Category A prison."

Robbie Smith, Court Reporter, Northern Echo

∼

Detective Constable Gary Dean

Postscript

Gary Dean won his case to have the family home sold. He received half of all the proceeds, including home furnishings, as well as access to his twin daughters, Ellie and Poppy, on alternate weekends and one mid-week evening.

With his share of the money, he put down the deposit on a modest, two bedroomed house where he could comfortably accommodate his children when they came to stay. This meant that he was able to re-establish the close bond they'd had before Shirley, now his ex wife, made it clear that she no longer wanted him in their lives.

When all of the attendant paperwork of the murder investigation was completed and the necessary preparations for Kelly's trial were concluded, he felt he was in a position, emotionally and mentally, to contact an organisation offering help specifically for male survivors of sexual abuse.

He was put in touch with a counsellor who was experienced in working with the victims and survivors of historical abuse. He was finally able to take the first steps on the long, often painful, path to dealing with the past trauma and exploring how the effects of it had impacted his adult life.

His outlook on life became more positive as he worked with his counsellor and his self-esteem grew, he was even contemplating taking his sergeant's exam. Life had really turned around for Gary Dean, with the help and support of his close friend and senior officer, Lottie Lockhart.

THE END

GLOSSARY OF SCOTS WORDS AND PHRASES

- A' - all
- A'right - alright
- Aboot - about
- Ah - I (first person singular)
- Aye - yes
- Bairns - children
- Blether - v. and n. To talk a lot, someone who talks a lot
- Brek - break
- Cannae - can't
- Cauld - cold
- Claes - clothes
- Couldnae - couldn't
- Dae - do
- Daein' - doing
- Didnae - didn't
- Doesnae - doesn't
- Fa' - fall
- Fae - from
- Gan - go (Northumberland)

- Gey - very
- Gonnae - going to
- Hame - home
- Havenae - haven't
- Heid - head
- Hoose - house
- Intae - into
- Jist - just
- Ken - know
- Laddie(s) - boy(s)
- Ma - my
- Nae - no or none
- Naw - no
- Navvy - labourer (originally on the railways 18thC)
- O' - of
- Oan - on
- Oot - out
- Ootside - outside
- Roond - round
- Sweetie wife - a man who likes to gossip/blether
- Tae - to or too
- Thae - those
- Thegither - together
- Tret - treat or treated (Northumberland and Scottish Borders)
- Wi' - with
- Wis - was
- Wisnae - wasn't
- Wummin - woman
- Wouldnae - wouldn't
- Ye - you
- Ye're - you're

ACKNOWLEDGMENTS

As always, I would like to thank my husband, Keith Race, for the time and commitment you have contributed in editing the manuscript and making this a better book to read. Your thoroughness and patience is very much appreciated.

My warm thanks also go to my friends and family who have encouraged and supported me on this journey, particularly Nell and Trish in Connecticut and Julie in New Zealand. You are always interested in the progress of my books and help to keep me on my toes. My thanks also go to Marie Robertson, Sam Thomas, Anne McKay and Jim Divine for their continued support.

ABOUT THE AUTHOR

Born in Edinburgh in 1954, Kay was educated at St Thomas Aquinas Senior Secondary School. She left school at the age of sixteen to work in the Civil Service.

A decade later, as a young mother, she graduated from Edinburgh University with a Joint Honours Degree in Sociology and Social Policy. Her undergraduate dissertation led her on to do postgraduate research into child abuse and neglect in nineteenth century Edinburgh.

Kay worked for many years as a psychotherapist and counsellor, specialising in working with survivors of child sexual abuse and domestic violence. She is retired now and lives in rural Northumberland with her husband and 10 year old whippet called Poppet.

Follow her on Twitter.com/KayRace2